Thank you
Karen!
Pam Jert

Sophomore Summer

by Jason Lambert

To the neighborhood of Riverton;
may you forever remain
a great place to grow up.

1

Sophomore year was good for Sam. Summer was looking even better. It began with his first rock concert. Bryan Adams rolled his *Into the Fire* tour into the Cumberland County Civic Center one Tuesday in June. Many times Sam had sat in those seats watching the Maine Mariners face off against the Hershey Bears, Binghamton Dusters, or some other American Hockey League team. The rock show though, was very different. Loud music and crowd energy overwhelmed him. Philly band The Hooters opened up, mixing two-year-old hits with new tunes. Bryan Adams followed the same formula. *Reckless* was still fresh and *Into the Fire* was in the top ten.

This would have been excitement enough, but what made the evening even better was speaking to Jessica Song for the first time. It wasn't much, a quick hello while finding his seat, but it was enough. Jessica was in his Geometry class. Her unique beauty entranced Sam. She was at the show with Stacy, another girl from Geometry. That's where Sam found himself the following afternoon, sitting next to Kat at the back of the room. Kat was her own thing; genie pants and hoop earrings made her stand out amongst the sea of jocks and preps. It was exactly what she was trying to do.

She pointed at his t-shirt. "How was the show?"

"Awesome!"

"Jessica and Stacy said it was good."

"I saw them there."

"They mentioned that."

A year ago, heck, six months ago, Sam would not have dared imagine speaking to a crush. Now, two girls had mentioned they had seen him at a rock show. The statement itself sounded cool, even if it could be read a million different ways. He supposed the girls could have thought he was a total geek; but maybe, just maybe, it was possible that one, or even both, thought that he was cute. Weight lost, inches grown, he was even developing a sense of style all his own; blue and white Reebok hi-tops, Levi's, and pastel Pipeline t-shirts shining out from pinstriped Oxfords halfway buttoned up.

Kat didn't care much for Bryan Adams. "I prefer the Cure," she said. "You should listen to them, and also the

Smiths."

Sam smiled, she had told him that before. "Maybe this summer," he said.

"I know, I know," Kat came back with, "it's Bryan Adams and Richard Marx for you."

To some degree, that was true. The style of the latter had become a template for Sam, who was letting his hair grow into a mullet. He also wore his new jean jacket everywhere.

Richard Marx may have been moving up the charts with a bullet, but one group was beyond all others to Sam. "Don't forget my favorite band."

"Oh Lord, Mr. Mister. You're incorrigible," Kat said in defeat. "At least you like U2."

"And REM."

"There is hope for you yet Sam Rinaldo."

The bell rang and the two stepped together into the hall. Sam spotted the goofy countenance of his neighborhood friend, Garrett, and made his way over to him.

"Talking to Kat eh," Garrett said. It was almost enough to make one suspect.

"Yeah, so," Sam said defensively.

"She likes you."

"Shut up."

Garrett let loose a stream of laughter. "She'd probably be cute if she tried to be a little more normal."

Sam agreed, "Probably." He had news. "Jessica Song told Kat she saw me at the concert."

"That doesn't mean anything."

The neighborhood trifecta became complete when Cal found them in the hustle and bustle. "You guys talking about me?" he asked, a little paranoid.

"No," Garrett said, "we're talking about Jessica Song."

"Shh," Sam pushed out.

Cal looked confused. He sometimes did. "Why were you talking about Jessica Song?"

Garrett looked over at an embarrassed Sam. "Somebody around here likes her."

"Who?" Cal asked before letting on that he got it. "Here she comes now!"

Sam caught Jessica's face in profile and those long braids falling onto her shoulders. He worried she had heard them. "Thanks a lot guys," he said as he began to Biology.

"Oh come on Sam, get over it," Garrett said, regaining the maturity he had momentarily lost.

Sam turned back and smiled. He pushed his head up to tell them all was cool.

Wasn't long before daydreams commenced in Biology. Sam thought about the concert, and about Jessica. His mind's eye focused on Bryan Adams playing songs Sam knew by heart. Jessica was next to him, they were holding hands. His imagination went further, now it was him up there holding an electric guitar.

"Sam," said Ms. Gallant. "It's your turn to read."

Everyone was looking at him. "Wh…where?" asked the daydreamer, setting off the class laugh track.

"Page three of the review packet, the second section, entitled organelles."

"Oh," Sam said. The daydream must have been going on for a while. He was still on the first page.

"*Stay* cool," one of the clowns up back said. There were a few chuckles.

Sam turned the page and found his bearing. "An organelle is the…"

He was up front on the bus when Jessica Song stepped on, her ears mostly covered by headphones. To the back she went. Sam wondered what was playing on her walkman. Bryan Adams maybe; Kat had said she liked U2. Sam wished he had the courage to go up back and sit next to her, but the waning insecurity of a husky puberty kept him silent. Jessica got off at the stop before Riverton School. His heart beat fast as she passed in high-cut acid-washed jeans and white Reeboks.

His stop was next. Into the late spring air he stepped beneath the familiar canopy of green trees arching over his street. Home was a good place to be, but Sam was starting to look to the further neighborhood. Garrett had his license now, and when his mother let him have the car, the three could explore the greater city. There was excitement in going to Lisa's Pizza by the Greyhound station, and out to the Maine Mall.

Sam went into his room. His stereo was waiting. He fingered through 45s until he found 'Kyrie' by Mr. Mister. Needle was placed on groove and soon synths were bubbling. Nobody was home so Sam turned it up and sang along.

The song hadn't quite reached the second chorus when he heard a loud, "Sam!"

His father was home from school. Sam hurriedly turned down the stereo. The kindly inclined middle-aged man was at the threshold of his son's room. "You know the Curtis's are elderly." he said, referring to the next door neighbors. "I'm sure they don't want to hear this racket."

Adolescence made it hard not to take everything personally. "I closed the window," Sam said in his defense.

Little brother Ben was smiling behind their father. Sam had a good relationship with his brother, but mostly they just stayed out of each other's way. Puberty had drawn a dividing line between them.

Headphones went on and soon the sonics of *The Joshua Tree* brought desert sunshine. It had come out at the very end of the winter. Sam understood what all the fuss was about one afternoon on the way home from a family ski trip. Pristine, expansive soundscapes gave soundtrack to perfect white landscapes passing at miles per hour. He took out his Geometry text and opened it in preparation for the final. He was good at writing proofs, but there was some trigonometry he needed to study. ∠ABC is 42° and side AB is 4.8 cm; find the measurements of the other angles. Sam couldn't focus for long. The cassette case was right there, and in it was the folded artwork with lyrics and credits. Sam skimmed through until he reached the producers; Brian Eno and Daniel Lanois. The boy's concept of how recordings were made was next to nil. All he had to go by was what he had seen on MTV; wood paneled rooms and men moving faders up and down. He dreamed that one day he would be in such a place, strumming a guitar and singing songs he had written. His closet door was partially open and there he could see the huge cardboard box that held his barely used guitar.

The smell of his mother's cooking filled the house, and soon the family was sitting around the table.

"How was your day at school?" was the question posed to both boys.

"Good," Sam said with no intention of elaborating. He couldn't say that girls in his Geometry class had mentioned they had seem him at the concert, or that he had been caught daydreaming in Biology. The former would have brought questions, the latter, remonstrances.

"I got a hundred on my Math test," Ben let out.

"Good job, " each parent said in turn.

The mind of the eldest son wandered. Sophomore year was coming to an end and Sam was ready for summer. He had no idea what was in store, but he imagined the possibility of seemingly endless days and what they may bring.

2

Driver's Ed started pretty much right after school was out. It hit Sam with a surprise; Jessica Song was there. He tried not to look at her too much that first day, but had a hard time of it. Sometimes she seemed to return his gaze, but he could never be sure. Insecurity caused him to see only the brown plastic bug-eyed glasses outlining his deep set eyes. He wondered what Jessica saw when she looked in the mirror. It could very well be that the things he liked best about her were what she was most self-conscious of; round moon light brown face, beautiful dark eyes, and a smile that moved her whole face upwards when it appeared.

That's what he meditated upon as he sat in his small, shadowed room with Richard Marx's debut cassette rolling through magnets and into headphones. He imagined himself walking up to Jessica after class, but when he played out this scenario, the only thing he could think to say was hello. He knew Jessica liked music; Kat had told him so. Kat had also told him that his crush had a crush of her own. It was part of the algebra that kept him from speaking to Jessica.

"Interested in anybody new?" Kat had asked one day as class was winding down.

The latest object of his affection was sitting up front. The room was big and busy enough to risk it. "Jessica Song," he said.

Kat's animated face smiled at him like he was a child. "Poor Sam," she said.

"Why?"

"Alas, the object of your affection has her heart set on another."

"Who?"

"Kevin Robichaud, they're in band together."

Sam had heard this kid was a good horn player, but that was about it. "Are they going out?"

"No, but Jessica has a big time crush on him."

Ever since that moment, Sam wondered how he measured up to Kevin Robichaud. With his slicked back hair, Robichaud always dressed formally, sometimes even in a tie. Maybe that's what girls liked. Sam had no idea. The class continued on as it usually did, Mr. Sayers went over proofs and theorems, and as Sam checked his answers, the possibility of Jessica Song liking him became a distant reality. There were certainly plenty of other girls at school, but it ain't easy when you have your heart set on one, and her heart is set on another. The brief exchange at the concert had rekindled the hope that something was possible.

Driver's Ed continued this upward trend until fate dealt him a blow. Classes were split and he and Jessica were separated. Opportunities to talk proved few and far between; there was one golden chance at the bike rack however. He undid the lock, turned his bike around, and there she was walking by. Instead of recalling the wave she gave him at the show, he remembered what Kat had told him about Kevin Robichaud and pedaled away.

Then, one sun-dappled afternoon, his father dropped him off in the back parking lot of Deering for driving practice.

"Pay attention," his father said sternly.

"I will Dad."

Sam closed the door behind him and saw Jessica standing at the student driver car. Besides the presence of the instructor, it would be just the two of them sharing a motor vehicle for an hour. She drove first. They left the back parking lot of Deering High School and drove around the city, ending up on Washington Avenue, near where driver's tests were taken.

"Turn left here," the paunchy middle aged instructor

said mechanically.

"Where?" she asked.

"Into the Rainbow Mall parking lot."

Jessica pulled the car into the vacant lot of the not long ago shuttered mall. It was Sam's turn to drive. He got out and took his place in the driver's seat. Each time he looked into the rearview mirror, there was Jessica, her head turned to street scenes of pizza places, gas stations, and post-war houses holding onto original shingles with varying success. Eventually, Sam caught Jessica's eye. It was at Woodford's Corner, with Dunkin' Donuts on the other side. He couldn't look long though, he had a road to watch.

His turn ended in the back parking lot of Deering High School. Each student driver had a car waiting. Jessica exited a step ahead of him, but Sam forced out, "Nice job driving," in a surge of bravery that surprised him.

His crush turned quick and smiled. That was it. Sam scored the interaction a failure and got into the front seat.

"How was the driving?" his father asked.

Flush with feelings of failure, Sam transmitted angst. "Fine," came out hurriedly.

"It's important for you to learn from these opportunities."

The interaction with Jessica had nothing to do with his father. "I know Dad," he said, less agitated this time.

Sam played the scene over in his mind; his words, her

silent smile. Obviously, she had no interest, otherwise she would have said something. It was after the second light at Morrill's Corner that his father said, "Your mother spoke with Gretchen Kincade. We are going to go down to Connecticut to visit them when you are done with driver's ed."

Going to the Kincade's meant only one thing to Sam; Karla. Families had been visiting each other every so many summers since before memory. The last visit though, was what resonated most in his mind. It was then when he saw MTV for the first time. Its rush of pictures moving through hits by the Police, Human League, and Culture Club intoxicated Sam. MTV however, was not the highlight of the trip. He, and little brother Ben, had slept in the same room as Karla and her little sister, Tina. Brothers shared a bed, the girls did too. It had been totally innocent of course, all pillow fights and a lot of giggling, but it had become mythical to Sam. After little siblings fell asleep, he and Karla talked deep into the night about music and school and the kind of things new adolescents talk about when first opening their eyes to the wide world before them. That was four years ago, Sam had come a long way.

Back in his room, he opened the drawers of his cassette cases one at a time to find a song that might fit what he was feeling. Instead of pulling out a tape and placing it in the deck, Sam thought of something. He opened his closet. There, amongst a cloister of baseball cards and memorabilia, was the guitar he had received for Christmas. He took it out of its box, where there also rested chord diagrams a family friend had drawn out for him. There was E minor, that was easy, full G and C were another story. Stretching his fingers was hard enough, but Sam had no way of knowing what order the chords were supposed to go in, or how long he was supposed to play them. He scribbled some words on notebook paper. Cars and parking lots appeared between blue lines, and there was Jessica in the rearview mirror. He struck that E minor chord. The guitar was definitely out of tune. It took his fumbling fingers more than a few seconds to find G.

Sam didn't realize his mother was standing in the doorway. "Glad to see you're finally using that guitar you asked for," she said.

"Ma," he replied, embarrassed at being caught with guard down. The guitar was put away. There was a song there, he knew it, but yet he did not.

Saturday morning meant busing tables at a little diner in Northgate Plaza. There were usually two waitresses working, plus Eleanor, who owned the place. In the kitchen was Sal, the head cook, and Luis, the Cuban refugee who was hard to understand sometimes. Of all of them though, his favorite by far was Stephanie. She was in her mid-twenties and pretty, with dirty blond hair pulled up into a ponytail. Dangling earrings led down to the rose pink waitress uniform she wore so well. She had become like the big sister Sam never had. He had been thinking about the drive with Jessica all morning, so when the early rush left but a few lingerers, he opened up to Stephanie, "There is a girl I like in my driver's ed class, well kind of in my class, there are two classes actually, but we drove together the other day."

"Oh yeah? What's her name?"

"Jessica."

"My best friend's name is Jessica," smiled Stephanie. "I like this girl already. Have you talked to her?"

"Not really that much."

"Why not?"

"I don't know, I'm shy I guess."

Stephanie chuckled. "Yes, you are."

"Plus I don't know what to say."

"Say anything."

"About what?"

"About your driver's ed class, about anything really."

Just then Steve walked in, he was Stephanie's boyfriend, and a drummer in a band that played around town. Stephanie said they sounded like REM, whose first hit had sprouted with spring. Steve was a good looking guy with curly hair longer than most people wore it. The young man took a seat at the counter and ordered a burger and fries from his girlfriend. Her trip to take the ticket to the kitchen window gave Steve a chance to ask Sam if he'd been playing his guitar.

"I took it out the other day," the teenager said.

"If you want to get better, you have to practice every-day."

Sam wanted to write songs almost more than anything, but was unable to envision a pathway to that end. Writing a song, or playing a song even, was very much a mystery. He didn't express that to Steve. Instead, he said, "I really like the new U2 album," and felt cool doing so.

"Yeah," the drummer said, "the space on that album is amazing. That's Lanois."

There was a table to clear. Sam left Steve and Stephanie to talk about whether they were going to her mother's later that afternoon.

Garrett's house was five minutes away by bike. That was where he found himself later on, playing computer baseball. Cal was there too, he usually was. The three of them had known each other going back to elementary school. Many baseball cards had passed between them. Many baseball board game leagues had been started, but rarely were they ever finished. *Baseball Strategy* was the first, then came *Statis Pro*, which simulated the game with cards that held statistical representations of actual players. The latter was their favorite by far. *Hardball* was their first foray into the realm of computer baseball games.

Garrett was one of those guys who was cocky, without it being evident why. He was tall and could eat up rebounds on the Riverton courts, but was never good enough to make the school team. His confidence could be handy in a pinch though, like the two times they tried to get into R-rated movies. Garrett went first and both times they got in.

Cal was mostly cool, but could be prickly at times, like on this eve when he reset the game of *Hardball* after Garrett scored four runs in the first inning.

"Hey, what are you doing?" Garrett asked angrily.

"I wasn't ready," was the answer.

"You weren't ready?"

"No, I was thinking about something else."

"What?"

Cal thought for a second. "Madonna," he let out.

"Madonna? Give me a break."

Sam laughed. He had certainly thought a lot about Madonna, especially after the 'Open Your Heart' video came out. Using that as an excuse to restart a game however, had never occurred to him.

Garrett collected himself. "Are you ready now?"

"Yes."

"You positive?"

"Yes," Cal repeated.

Sure enough, the next song on FM 103 was, 'Who's That Girl', Madonna's summer single. Normally Garrett would change it to WBLM immediately, but he wanted to savor the moment. "Should we wait until the song is over before starting?"

"Shut up. Let's play."

"A Madonna delay," Sam said, laughing as he fell back on his friend's bed.

The last day of driver's ed soon came. Classes were combined for the final. With so many people packed in the room, Sam could not see Jessica from where he was sitting. Stapled papers were passed back down the rows. The questions were easy and Sam was pretty certain he did well. Just to make sure, he went back through the questions one by one. Getting a permit was of the utmost importance, as it was for everybody else in that room. Once he was confident all his answers were correct, Sam stood and looked toward where Jessica had been sitting, she was no longer there.

3

Headphones filled with sound as the family drove down to Connecticut. The Hooters latest cassette, *One Way Home,* was in Sam's walkman. The songs were certainly earnest, and catchy too. As he looked out at trees lining 95, Sam attempted to sort through the excitement of seeing Karla. He imagined them talking, little siblings off someplace else. Then, at some point, there would be a lot of kissing. Sam knew the likelihood of that fantasy coming true was pretty much next to nil, but it didn't hurt to dream as the car rolled down 95.

First to greet them in the driveway was Gretchen. She used to be a hippy, and in some ways still was, aging gracefully with long blond hair flecked with gray. Her husband, Andrew, stood tall beside her. With the thick beard, he looked like a biblical character. Tina was the first sister out of the house. Sam could tell Ben thought she was cute, with her brown hair in a bob. A smile lit up his brother's face, and after hugging the adults, the younger siblings were on their way to the backyard swing set.

Gretchen hugged the older brother. "You look great Sam. It's been so long."

The adolescent was too embarrassed to say thank you, so he just smiled. He answered Gretchen's questions mechanically; school was fine, he was going to be a junior in the fall.

The screen door snapped back. Sam saw Karla stepping down porch stairs in bare feet, white shorts, and a black Tears for Fears t-shirt. Four years had not changed her as much as it had him, but she was fuller now, in a good way. Her hair was longer too, but still that summer shade of blond he remembered.

Karla came right over and hugged his mother and father. In time, the four who remained in the driveway joined the younger two in the backyard. The Kincades lived near the ocean's edge. Andrew had quit his job with a firm in the city to become a lobsterman. While parents talked Iran-Contra on the deck, the kids went to the picnic table in the backyard. Sisters sat on one side, brothers on the other. "We finally got MTV two years ago," Sam said, remembering how mesmerized he had been back in '83.

"You get things slow up there," Karla observed.

It was true. "Yeah, we do."

"What have you been listening to?"

"I like Tears for Fears," he said pointing at her shirt, "and I like the new U2 album."

"Me too."

Sam thought about repeating what Steve had said about Lanois, but Ben jumped in, "I think that album is boring."

"You don't know what you're talking about," Sam said before sharing a grin of understanding with Karla.

Conversation turned to television shows. It was the golden age of sit-coms.

"*Family Ties* is my favorite," Karla said.

"Mine too," replied Sam.

Karla looked at her little sister. "Tina's favorite is *Growing Pains*. She's in love with Kirk Cameron."

"No I'm not," hissed little sister.

Karla looked at Sam and dimple smiled. That was all it took to set his heart a-flutter.

It was from the deck of the lobster boat that they watched the slow decline of sunshine into blue orange yellow twilight. Andrew was piloting to one of his buoys. This was not a work trip, but rather one arranged for the enjoyment of guests.

Wind in his face, Sam stared out across oceans vast. He took off his glasses and pulled sea air into his lungs. The corner of his eye caught Karla looking at him.

"What do you think?" she asked.

Sam moved nearer to her on the deck. "It's pretty cool."

Karla smiled. "Yeah, but it's hard work."

"Pulling up the traps?"

"I'm sure you'll get to try it, my dad left a few for you guys."

Andrew overheard. "I was trying to make it seem natural Karla," he said with pretend exasperation.

"Sorry Dad."

Sam turned his attention to Ben, who was standing near Tina. Brothers exchanged a knowing glance. Sam felt a touch on his shoulder. It was Karla. "Can I wear your jacket?" she asked. "It gets cold when the sun goes down."

"Sure," the boy said blissfully as he handed it to her.

Sam looked at Karla in his Levi's Trucker jacket. It was too big, but certainly looked good on her.

"Okay," Andrew announced. "We're coming up on the traps."

Inertia landed them alongside a buoy bobbing on the low waves. Andrew grabbed a long pole and pulled the buoy to the side of the boat. The lobsterman glanced over his shoulder. "Okay men, let's get working."

The rope was thick and heavy as Sam and his brother slowly lifted it from the depths. "How far down is the trap?" asked their father.

"About sixty-five feet," came the answer.

It was getting tougher, but they had to persevere for there were females of interest watching. Just as Sam was ready to ask for help, the trap became visible through the lapping waves.

Andrew came up behind them. "You guys are hired," he said as he assisted in pulling the trap onto the deck. Five lobsters were inside. The lobsterman worked quick. Two were tossed back into the ocean. The other three were placed in a bucket of sea water. There was one more stop to make. The trap came up quick this time. There were four more lobsters inside.

"That's tomorrow's dinner," Andrew announced as he started the motor to begin back to shore.

Sam moved to where Karla was sitting. "The traps are heavy, aren't they?" she asked.

"You could say that," he said.

Karla smiled back at him. She knew he was trying to be cool. He totally knew he was too.

There would be no sleeping in the same room this year. Parents did not want to take a chance on the quotient of adolescence. The girls slept in their attic room, and the boys got a cot and couch in the living room. It was late and Sam lay with headphones over his ears, moving his radio dial slowly from left to right. City stations appeared out of static; there was late night jazz and underground hip-hop, the DJ said it was Man Parrish; there was guitar sludge, and urban stations playing Run-DMC songs Sam had never heard before. Further up the dial he went until his search stumbled on a song by the Outfield. He fell asleep as guitars and harmonies filled headspace.

Morning came with synth horn sunlight blaring through bay windows. Sam's first thought was Karla, upstairs, probably still sleeping. Soon enough she descended. The white shorts of the day before had given way to cut off jeans and a Cure t-shirt with big red lips.

Families gathered for breakfast. On the table there were pancakes, fresh fruit, juice, and milk, and on the other side of it all was Karla. Parents talked of mutual friends, and of family. Sam didn't mind listening as Karla's bare feet scraped the hard wood floor near his white tube socks.

Gretchen looked at her daughters. "Why don't you take the boys downstairs to play pool?"

To the basement they went. In the center of the wood paneled room was a pool table. Colorful mid-century shelving filled the far wall, where records leaned neatly upon one another. Sam went right over. Most of the vinyl was from the sixties: the Beatles, the Stones, Sly, and a bunch of singer songwriters. The lower partition belonged to the kids: Duran Duran, the Cure, the Police.

"Have you ever heard of the Smiths?"

Kat had mentioned them. "I've heard of them, but

never listened to them."

"I love the Smiths," Tina said from across the room.

Karla pulled out a record and put it on the turntable. For the first time, Sam heard the darting melodic cadences of Johnny Marr's guitar and Morrissey's ghostly croon. It was certainly unlike anything he had heard on pop radio.

The four of them played pool, but not very well. Sam and Karla got talking local slang. "*Stay* cool is one at my school," Sam said. "It's supposed to be sarcastic, like meaning not really cool."

"I like that. Mind if I try it around here?"

"Go ahead," Sam said, hoping it would spread.

"Stay cool," she said, flat.

"Hang on the *stay*."

"*Stay* cool."

It was close enough.

Parting was such sweet sorrow. Families stood in the driveway, delaying the inevitable. Sam had already decided he was going to hug Karla, so when the moment came, he did just that. It was reciprocated. "*Stay* cool," she said to him.

"You too."

Sam climbed into the familiar back seat next to his brother. Headphones went on. Sam turned to the window. Karla was waiting for him to look. They smiled at each other as the car pulled away.

4

Soon enough, Sam was back at the diner, bussing tables and pouring coffee. Stephanie was working that Saturday, she almost always was. Morning rush was normal busy until its usual lull. His favorite waitress leaned next to him at the counter. "Did you ever talk to that girl in driver's ed?"

Sam looked down at Stephanie's pink Converse sneakers with yellow pastel laces tied round her heel. "No," he answered honestly.

"Oh no, you probably won't see her again until school starts."

That was likely true, but there was someone else fresh on his mind. "We were just down in Connecticut visiting friends who have a daughter my age."

"Look at you," gushed Stephanie.

Sam blushed and looked around to see if anybody had heard. The place was empty except for the old ladies who barely tip. They were prattling on about something in the booth near the window.

"Her name is Karla, and she loves music," Sam said quietly.

"And so do you."

Sam nodded

"Will you see her again?"

Reality was that it had been four years since he had last seen her. There was no telling when he would see her again. That truth brought back the disappointment of not talking to Jessica. He told that to Stephanie.

"School will be starting sooner than you think."

Stephanie was right, but he did not want to rush it along. There was still a summer filled with baseball cards and *Hardball* and adventures with his friends. It was up in Garrett's room, while he and Cal were playing *Hardball*, that Sam told them about Karla with a K.

"Is this the one you used to brag about sleeping in the same room with?" Garrett asked skeptically.

Cal smirked. "Yeah, until we found out younger siblings were sleeping in the same room."

Laughter resounded.

"Shut up," Sam said.

Cal cast a sly eye toward him. "Did you get some this

time?"

Sam wasn't going to lie about such a thing, but telling them she wore his coat on the lobster boat would hardly impress this audience. "Parents were around," he answered.

"So."

Sam was becoming incensed. "So? Give me a break," he let out. "When was the last time you kissed a girl Cal?"

"Last summer, up at Sebago."

Sam didn't believe him. "Yeah, right."

Garrett got a pass on this one. He had accompanied some junior in his Algebra II class to her prom. Others there confirmed making out had taken place. Cal and Garrett sank back into the game and the discussion ended there. AC/DC was in the cassette deck, as it often was. Sam wondered what they would say if he popped the Smiths into the well worn deck. The thought of their imagined reaction made him smile.

It was a boring weekday afternoon when Sam decided to walk through the short woods behind his house and over to Riverton School. Directly before him was the ball field, and there were the basketball courts where the boys spent a lot of time playing and arguing in their high-tops.

"That was a foul," one would inevitably say.

"I didn't even touch you!" was what the accused usually replied.

"Look, you can see where my arm is red!"

Then, sure enough, the third would be called in to make a decision which would evidently make one party unhappy, and the arguing would commence yet again.

Sam had no particular destination in mind. Maybe he would go to the gym and see if people he knew were working. He walked down that way, but the gym door was locked. He decided to proceed back down the hall, through library doors and into space he had known for almost all memory. To his right were the sports books he often gravitated toward. Today though, he walked right past, to the music section. There wasn't much there, couple shelves worth of books about classical, jazz, and musicals. There was also a decade-old history of rock music. Sam picked it up and turned the pages to see photos of Elvis Presley, The Beatles, Jimi Hendrix, and then there was Bowie and other seventies glam bands with their platform boots and androgyny.

Sam turned and there was Jessica Song. He couldn't let another chance slip away. Heart beat hard inside his chest as he felt himself moving toward her without knowing what to say. Jessica was picking up a book from the counter when he reached her.

"Hello," he said.

"Hi," came the reply.

Sam was in a conversation with Jessica Song, for real. "We drove together."

"I remember."

"And Geometry."

"Mister Sayers," she said with a laugh.

"Both funny and boring."

"I'd say more boring than funny."

The conversation continued on about school and driver's ed. Sam decided to press his luck. "If you want I could walk you home."

Jessica shrugged her shoulders. "Sure, I guess."

It wasn't the ringing endorsement he was hoping for, but it would do. They began up the stairs together.

"You didn't take out any books?" she asked.

Now he felt bad he hadn't. "Not today." He looked down to the book she held in her hand. "What did you get?"

"*Jane Eyre*. My grandmother loves this book. Now that driver's ed is over, it's my back to school reading assignment."

Sam was glad his parents didn't give him one of those.

Jessica looked even more beautiful in the bright sunshine. Her face had peaceful gravity, black eyebrows highlighted unfurling lashes and dark eyes. Jessica caught him admiring, and smiled. "What do you like to read?" she asked.

Books about baseball didn't sound very cool so he said, "I like to read about music."

"What type of music?"

"Rock, and pop too."

Jessica nodded her approval and fell into silence as they walked past the fire station. Home was one way for him, her, another. "It's been nice walking with you," she said.

Words in past tense hit him hard. He worried he had done something wrong. "Okay," was all that came out.

"I guess you can call me if you want."

Deflation to elation had never been quicker. "Sure," he said, trying very hard to stay cool.

Jessica's pink painted nails reached down into a tiny black purse to pull out a pad and pen. She wrote the number out and gave it to him. "Bye," she said as she moved to catch the green walk light visible through bright sunshine.

Sam looked down at the paper; there, in blue ink, were seven digits and a name. He wondered what would happen when he dialed. Would she answer? Would someone else pick up the phone? Or would it just keep ringing?

Sam took out the number when he reached his room. He couldn't keep it on his dresser. Ben might find it, or his mother might see the numbers written in neat script and then there would be questions that would feel like an interrogation. Sam looked around his room. His closet door was open and therein sat the trapezoidal box that held his guitar. Sam folded the paper once and put it inside.

The number haunted him. One day passed, then another, and finally no one was home. He took the paper out from its hiding place and made his way to the kitchen where the heavy green phone waited. He took the hand piece off its cradle and dialed one digit at a time. His heart jumped into his throat when it started to ring; one, two, three times it went, four times, five. He removed the receiver from his ear and hung up.

There was nothing for it; all that risk he had taken, all the nerves bundled up inside, all the desire as yet undefined, went for nought. Sam went into his room and put the number back into the guitar case, pausing for a moment before the instrument. He imagined a teenage vision of himself as a rock star, hammering chords hard enough to shake the foundations of something. Sam took the guitar out of its case and started raggedly strumming an E minor chord. He was out of tune, there was no doubt about that, but he heard something in the blurry haze of notes.

Ben suddenly appeared at the door. "You're out of tune you know."

Little brother was standing there with a grin. The elder was hurt but didn't say anything. Ben was right, but to hear that fact spoken aloud was all the discouragement Sam needed to return the guitar to its case.

Saturday was slow at the diner. It was full bright summer and people were likely at the beach. Sam was looking forward to telling Stephanie about the phone number and how he had tried to call. She was working, but was not her usual self. Her step was not as spirited, and while still polite to everybody, her words were spoken without the usual enthusiasm. Sam wanted to ask if she was okay, but he was just a kid, well, an adolescent, and felt out of place doing so.

The reason for her state of mind became evident later that morning when Steve came down the walk with his head down. The restaurant was pretty empty when he maneuvered through two glass doors and meekly stood at the hostess station.

Stephanie was pouring coffee to one of the little old ladies who barely tip. She received their gratitude graciously, then acted so cool as she went over to her boyfriend with the nearly full pot of hot coffee in her hand. "What are you doing here Steven?"

"I wanted to see you."

The old ladies tilted their ears to listen, a few other patrons also tuned into the drama being played out before them.

"This is not the place to talk," Stephanie told him in no uncertain terms.

"Can I call you?"

Stephanie stood silent. No doubt many in the diner were wondering about the pot of coffee in her hand. Stephanie's eyes glazed over for a second, then she let out an exasperated chuckle before turning and walking back toward the counter, safely placing the pot of coffee on its burner. Sam watched her glide through the swinging doors and into the kitchen. Mindy, one of the other waitresses, followed behind.

Steve stood there for a few seconds, hoping Stephanie would appear again. The young man looked at the adolescent. Sam shrugged his shoulders. Steve allowed himself a humbled grin before turning and walking back into the bright sunshine. The boy thought about his walk with Jessica. He wondered if falling in love inevitably led to public displays of something gone wrong.

"Is he gone?" came from behind him. It was Stephanie slowly advancing out from the kitchen. Sam nodded and the waitress returned to the quiet dining room. "Promise me something," she said.

Sam blushed. "Okay."

"Promise me that when you get older you won't stop being a nice guy."

Sam hardly thought of himself as a full-fledged guy, but he said, "I'll try."

Eleanor walked up to him. She was very elegant, though well into middle age. As far as bosses go, she was easy, yet never afraid to ask when something needed to be done. "Would you mind helping out Luis with the dishes? He's swamped."

Sam went through double doors to find Luis at the dishwashing station. The machine had broken down. It took both Sal and Eleanor to help Luis get it fixed. This misfortune had left three bussing tubs filled with dirty dishes to be sorted and cleaned. Luis stood there overwhelmed amidst the mess. His white and blue mesh baseball cap was tilted at an odd angle on his fluffy afro.

"I'm here to help you Luis," Sam said.

"You help me?"

"Yes."

Luis smiled and straightened his cap. He looked up and made the sign of the cross before closing his hands in prayer. "Thank you," he said.

Luis rinsed dishes with the hose sprayer that hung over the roaring disposal. He then handed each to Sam, who put them into a big gray dishwashing tray. The cooks had the small transistor cranking out classic rock on WBLM.

Sam wondered if Luis had ever experienced anything like what he had just witnessed between Stephanie and Steve, or if he knew what it was like to feel nervous about calling a girl. He wanted to ask, but Sam was pretty sure it would be lost in translation. So there he stood next to the steaming dishwashing machine listening to 'Sweet Child O' Mine' blast out over the radio.

5

Upstairs in Garrett's room, the usual debate around music ended with an agreement to listen to the top requests of the day on the pop radio station. "It's time for the top nine at nine," the DJ said, "which means it's also time to give away two tickets to Huey Lewis and the News at the Ballpark to the seventh caller."

Garrett sprung into action and pushed the corresponding touch tones. "Busy," he said.

"Try again," urged Sam.

He did. "It's ringing."

The DJ answered the call over the radio. "FM 103," he said.

Suddenly, Garrett's voice was on the air. "Hello," he said, a bit confused.

"Congratulations, you are the correct caller!"

"Awesome!"

"Do you know what you won?"

"Two tickets to Huey Lewis."

"That's right. Where are you calling from?"

"Portland."

The other boys whooped it up in the background.

"Sounds like you got some rowdy friends."

"You could say that."

High fives went all around. It was decided they would split the cost for the third ticket so they all could go to the show. Cal and Garrett started their game. Sam looked out the open dormer window and watched cars and trucks rushing by on 95 as the sun set behind them. As vehicles whooshed past, he wondered where each was going. It all seemed like a Springsteen song. He thought of his guitar and the few chords he had managed to play.

"I tried to call Jessica Song this week," Sam said.

"Why?" muttered Cal between pitches.

"Because I like her."

"You like everybody," Garrett said.

Sure, he had a penchant for crushes, but what was so bad about that? Garrett had crushes sometimes, Cal not so much. "I don't like everybody," Sam said in defense.

"Pretty much," Cal came back with. He swung and missed Garrett's simulated fastball. "I heard she's like in love with Kevin Robichaud."

There it was again. He had almost forgotten. His heart dropped for a moment, but it rose as he thought how he had walked with her from the library and told them so.

"That doesn't mean she likes you," Garrett said.

"I got her phone number."

That was the last word. His friends were paying too much attention to the game, and were maybe a little jealous. Sam turned back to 95, the sun was completely behind the highway now and its place had been taken by darkness pushing down. He thought of Karla on that lobster boat in waters a few states away. Sam wondered if she was thinking of him.

Stephanie was back to her normal self on Saturday, full of energy and joking with the regulars. They respected her. She was funny, and put up with men well on the other side of middle age calling her 'hon' all the time. Sam wanted to ask what was going on with Steve, but didn't quite dare. It was adult business. He told her about his life because she knew about growing up.

"Have you run into that girl from the neighborhood?" she asked later that shift.

As a matter of fact, he had. Sam told Stephanie about the library, the phone number, the unanswered call.

"You have to call her again," insisted Stephanie.

"But people have told me she is in love with Kevin Robichaud."

"Who's that?"

"This kid at school."

"She's what, fifteen? sixteen?"

Sam supposed so.

"Is she dating this guy?"

Sam shrugged his shoulders.

"A crush and being in love are two very different things."

"I guess."

"She let you walk her home."

That was true, almost. It hadn't been all the way home. He didn't bother correcting her.

Stephanie continued. "What's this kid got that you don't?"

"He plays saxophone in the band."

"So, you play guitar."

"I know like one chord."

"You'll learn more."

It was no use, she wasn't going to let him off that easy. "Okay, I promise to call her."

Stephanie smiled.

"Miss," said one of the small tippers from across the room.

Stephanie grabbed the orange-topped pot of coffee and walked over to the table by the window. Sam looked at the scene before him; the joint was practically empty, and in an hour, the whole afternoon was his. He thought about what he might do: a bike ride was likely, maybe some basketball, he almost forgot he had some baseball cards that needed sorting. He thought of Jessica and her phone number sitting in the bottom of the box that held his guitar.

That early evening, under the burnt orange darkening twilight, the boys rode their bikes up Allen Avenue to Northgate for some candlepin bowling. The place was buzzing. People of all ages were there, but it was mostly younger kids and their parents.

The sounds of balls rolling down lanes and striking pins echoed throughout the space. They were assigned lane fifteen. Garrett took the scoresheet and sat down to write their names in neat cursive.

"I want to go first," Cal said, putting on his bowling shoes with haste.

"Fine," was the reply. "Sam, do you want to go second?"

"Sure."

It was settled.

The lane was turned on and pins were set by the machine. Cal went up to choose his ball. He picked up each and weighed them in his hand. Then he went through the motion of throwing as an additional test.

"Would you start already?" asked an impatient Garrett.

"I have to find my lucky ball."

Garrett just shook his head.

"Okay," Cal said, holding up a black ball speckled white and yellow. "This is my lucky ball. Nobody else can use it."

Sam turned from the dialogue and looked across the lanes. He saw Stephanie down the other end. She looked different without her work clothes. Instead of the rose pink waitress uniform, she was wearing high cut tapered jeans, into which a pastel t-shirt was tucked. Her hair was straight down below her shoulders, not in the usual flopping ponytail. Mindy from work was there too, and so was some other young woman Sam didn't know.

"Your turn Sam," Garrett said.

Sam stepped up. He waited for the last used ball to jet up from the tunnel and take its place at rest next to the others.

"That's my ball," Cal said.

"Are you serious?" Garrett asked.

"What's wrong with having a lucky ball?"

Garrett did not bother to answer.

Sam found another ball just as fine. He took his position with it cupped in his hands, almost like a prayer. Into the wind-up he went, then let the ball unfurl fast as possible while still retaining control. It rolled toward the center, and seven pins fell. Two pins to the left and one to the right remained. He took aim for the two on the left with his next shot, but only hit one. His third ball missed altogether.

"Eight," he called to Garrett, who wrote it down.

Sam looked toward Stephanie. Her smile connected them across the lanes. Sam waved. She started walking towards him. He met her in front of the counter, where a family was returning their shoes.

"Hey," she said, "long time no see."

It had been only a few hours since work ended. Talking to Stephanie again in the middle of the alley felt strange, but familiar too.

"I didn't know you liked to go bowling," he said.

"Just out with the girls for some Saturday night fun."

"Me too," Sam said, "out with the boys I mean."

"I know what you mean," Stephanie smiled. "Well, I just wanted to say hello. Have a fun night Sam."

"You too."

Sam turned and started to walk back. Jessica's friend Stacy and some girls from school were sitting around on hard blue plastic chairs in front of lane seven. He did not see Jessica with them, but couldn't help wonder if she was there, somewhere.

"It's your turn Sam," Cal impatiently informed him upon his return.

He took his spot. Sam did his best to shake it off and focus on the task at hand. His first throw veered more to the left than he would have liked and only two pins fell.

His other two tries knocked down three on the other side. Not his best turn. He sat back down next to Garrett.

"Five," he said.

His friend wrote down the score and turned to him. "Who was that you were talking to?"

"Stephanie, from work."

"You work with her?"

Sam nodded.

"You're lucky."

Sam knew he was. He glanced toward where the girls from school were bowling. Stacy and another girl were looking at him and whispering. They started giggling.

Embarrassed, Sam turned to watch Garrett. It was his second shot. He knocked down the remaining pins for a spare. "Yes!" he exclaimed as he punched his fist in the air.

The peak of excitement had passed. It was a fun time nonetheless. Sam's game improved. He almost beat Garrett in the third string. By that time, Cal's lucky ball had long been abandoned. Sam occasionally looked over to Stacy and the girls from school. Jessica never appeared. Stephanie waved to him from across the lanes when she left, so did Mindy. It wasn't too much longer before the boys were back on their bikes, riding home under the remaining ribbons of summer twilight.

6

Sam gathered the courage to call Jessica the very next day. Touch tone phone starting ringing on the other end; one, two, three, then, "Hello?" questioned an older woman's voice.

"Hello. Is Jessica there?"

"Yes. Can I tell her who's calling?"

"Sam."

The phone on the other end was put down. Sam's heart was beating hard, blood rushed to his head.

"Hello," came a voice Sam recognized.

"Jessica?"

"Yes."

"It's Sam from Geometry."

"Yeah, hi."

"How are you?"

"Good."

He was struggling for words and looked out his window. "It's beautiful outside."

"Yes it is."

"Do you want to hang out?"

"Sure," she said, and with that, Sam's heart did a somersault inside its cage.

"What do you want to do?"

"How about a walk?" she suggested. "I'll meet you at the library."

Ten minutes later that's exactly where Sam was. He headed across the room to the periodicals, carefully listening for the door above. It opened. A pretty young mother with two little children entered. The oldest was allowed to walk down the steps all by himself. Sam couldn't help but smile. The door opened again. Jessica was at the top of the stairs. Her dark hair was pulled back in a straight ponytail. Sam was transfixed; she was there to meet him, but had books to bring to the counter first. "I'm returning these for my grandmother," she said.

"Thank you Jessica," replied the librarian.

"You're welcome Mrs. Marion," Jessica said before turning to Sam. "Are you ready?"

Yes, he was.

They exited the library and pushed through large metal doors. Summer was there when they stepped outside, as were the vast back fields past the nearly empty parking lot. Further out were the brightly painted tennis courts and the softball fields; one for girl's Little League, and the one behind for the men's league, with its light towers that illuminated summer nights. Sam could hear their revelry through his open window. The soccer fields were out there too, then the woods, out of which grew radio towers blinking slow incessant rhythms.

"Have you ever been down to the radio towers?" she asked.

"Yeah."

"What's it like?"

"A little swampy, but there are planks you can walk on."

"Do you remember how to get out there?"

Sam looked out over fields and trees and pointed where they needed to go. "We have to get over to Lane Avenue first," he said, leading her past the little league field filled with minor glories of the not so distant past. He didn't tell her about any of that as they began through the woods and past the old Little League Three scoreboard, an artifact rusting amidst the tangles. The boys had once tried to carry it out in vain.

"When did you go out to the radio towers?" she asked.

"Last summer. Me and my friends rode our bikes down to the end of the dirt road and walked from there."

They were at the dirt road now. Sam was nervous all of a sudden. Hands went into pockets as he looked up at three radio towers blinking against the perfect blue sky.

Near the small white building was the ladder that led to the planks and towers. They climbed rungs one at a time until they were five feet above wetlands now dry in the summer sun. Tall grasses reached toward them in vain.

Jessica looked down, pushing straight hair out of her face with pink fingernails. "Do you think there are snakes down there?" she asked.

"Hard to say," Sam replied honestly.

If there were any, they would be small and colorful and not at all seeking interaction with two teenagers, nor anyone else for that matter. He looked up to Warren Avenue and spotted the baseball card shop destined to fail amidst corrugated-steel warehouses. It had once been a dream of his to have his own card shop someday; to spend his day surrounded by memorabilia, sorting through cards as he had done through the dark storms of puberty. None of this he dared say to Jessica. He remained quiet as adolescent steps led them to the base of one of the radio towers. Sam looked up to its blinking red beacon flashing against the clear blue sky. There was a ladder that climbed to the top. The view must be amazing from there Sam thought. Casco Bay and the Atlantic Ocean were to the immediate east, mountains further to the west.

Jessica stopped and sat when they were about half way out. Sam followed her down onto the planks and together they looked across tall grass and shrubs alternating up to the road and cars passing in the distance.

"Warren Avenue is kind of pretty from here," observed Jessica. "All the cars rushing places, and the buildings with people working."

Sam smiled. It was a cool thing to say, he imagined turning the sentiment into a song. There was silence for a few seconds before Jessica turned to him. "What's your favorite place?" she ventured.

"My room," is what came out.

"Me too," she said happily. "What do you like so much about your room?"

Sam thought about the barely used guitar. To say that was the reason he liked his room best would be exaggerating. There were all the baseball cards in his closet, a shrine that reached nearly to the ceiling. A year ago he would have said that without hesitation, but not anymore. "My music," he said instead.

"You really like music?"

"Yeah."

"Me too," she said, turning one side of her head upward and looking toward the sky as if searching for a thought. "I like my room best because that's where I read."

Sam liked to read. Not as much as he used to, but he

still did it every day. It wasn't as formal as it used to be. There were no longer tomes on the history of the American League, or analytical treatises on season's past. Magazines were his thing now. He still read *Sporting News*, but had been buying *Billboard* and *Rolling Stone* too.

"You're friends with Kat?" Jessica asked.

Sam wasn't sure exactly how to handle this one. "Yeah," he admitted.

Jessica let out a little laugh. "I like Kat," was her response.

"Kat's pretty cool I guess, except she always gives me a hard time."

"That's Kat, she's definitely not afraid to be herself. I wish I was more like her."

It was both weird and kind of cool to Sam that someone wanted to be more like Kat, whose stubbornness of self got her branded a granola or worse by the conforming multitude. School had a clear social structure. Jocks and preps were on the top; below them were the heavy metal skids, then there were the granolas, looked down upon by the rest. Really though, granolas were the cutting edge, harbingers of the alternative revolution to come.

"Do you think you're not yourself?" asked Sam.

Jessica looked out toward Warren Avenue. "My problem is I don't think I know who I really am."

Sam didn't know what to say. What did it really mean

to be yourself? He had never thought about it in such high stakes terms. He thought of his own life. Was it baseball cards and cassette tapes that made him who he was? Family and friends?

The cool whispers of sea breezes told them the afternoon was passing. "We probably should be getting back," Jessica said.

Sam nodded and got to his feet. He held out his hand to her. It remained in his own as they retraced their steps back to the road. When they reached the school, they passed blue pods whose plastic windows had been burned black by burnouts. The upper playground was soon before them. In its elevated center stood a wooden arch with handles climbing to a height from which there hung a tire swing.

"I love this playground," Jessica said.

"It seems like such a long time ago since recess."

"I know."

"I used to be afraid to climb the arch."

"Me too," Jessica said as she stepped toward the tire swing. She grabbed hold of the chain. "Will you give me a push?"

Sam watched as she climbed up into the tire and hung her legs over. Her head full of black hair leaned back. He pulled the chains and the backward motion of the swing left her ponytail near his face. She smelled of summertime.

He let go the swing and soon Jessica was in random pendulum motion. Her head fell back and she laughed to the blue sky and its wispy clouds. "It's been so long since I did this," she said, reaching her acid washed jeans and white Reeboks toward the sky.

Sam couldn't help but smile. "Do you want me to push you again?" he asked.

"Yeah."

He grabbed the swing and pulled it in close. Then, he let it go, sending Jessica twirling through the air again in an unpredictable rotation that made her laugh out loud. The old playground never felt so good.

"Okay, okay, I'm starting to get dizzy," she said, still laughing.

Sam grabbed the twirling swing. It led him back across the depression formed by countless dragging feet. Eventually, the tire came to a halt and Jessica was able to dismount. "Oh my God," she said, "that was so much fun. I need to sit for a minute though."

Sam pointed to the large concrete drainage pipe repurposed as a spot for kids to huddle. "Good idea," she said and climbed in. He followed and there they sat together, staring at the graffiti. Both felt a rush of memory. "I remember climbing in here at recess, no boys allowed," Jessica said with a laugh.

"It seemed so much bigger then."

"Yeah, you could fit like four people."

"Not anymore."

They had grown up less than a half mile away from each other, but Geometry was the first time they had been in the same class. He had gazed at her across a classroom, and now, here she was sitting next to him. Sam wanted to kiss her; but what if he tried and failed? What if she rejected him? It would ruin this near perfect day. Cal and Garrett would surely ask how far he got. If he told them he and Jessica had only held hands, there would be teasing for sure. He looked over at Jessica. Her searching eyes seemed to be pondering something.

"Do you have brothers and sisters?" she asked Sam.

"I have a little brother."

"Do you get along?"

"Yeah, we don't really talk too much, but it's not because we don't like each other."

Jessica thought it over. She looked straight ahead, where a couple had carved their initials in the concrete. "I have a little brother, well half-brother, that I have never met," she said.

That idea seemed so foreign to Sam. How could somebody have a brother they had never met? She had told him she lived with her grandmother. Dots were connecting, but the form was hazy. Sam wasn't sure what to say.

"I'm going to New York to meet him next week. I'm

kind of nervous." Jessica tried to explain, "My father had to go away," she said simply, "and now my mother is in New York with her new husband. She wants me to come live with them."

Sam's family had always been stable. He knew people at school whose parents were divorced, but it had not yet reached the inner circle of his life. He could think of only one question, "Are you going to move?"

Jessica looked over to him. "I really don't know," she replied. "My grandmother raised me and I can't imagine being without her."

Sam tried to picture his Nana raising him. A smile came first, but the lonely feeling of being without two parents and a little brother overtook him.

"I'm sorry, I'm talking about myself," Jessica said.

"It's okay," Sam replied, smoother than he knew he could.

Jessica turned her arm to look at her thin wrist watch, "I probably should be heading back."

Sam knew this moment would come, but that didn't stop him from being disappointed. He climbed out the concrete circumference after her. They ascended the rest of the hill and walked past the old graveyard.

She hugged him when they reached the fire station. It paralyzed Sam like a cartoon character.

"Thank you for listening," she said, pulling away from

him with a smile.

Sam walked back past the graveyard and traced familiar steps. He had spent part of the afternoon with Jessica Song, who very soon would be going away to meet her brother for the first time. All this was pinging in his head when he walked into the kitchen. It smelled good. His mother was cooking dinner. "Hi Sam," she said.

"Hi Ma."

"Were you out on your bike?"

He couldn't bring himself to tell her about Jessica and their journey to the planks of the radio towers.

"Just out walking," he said to avoid a lie.

"Gretchen Kincade called earlier this afternoon. They are coming up Labor Day weekend with the girls. You and your brother will have to sleep in the living room."

Sam's brain was already swirling, now it was sent aloft. Karla would be staying at his house. He continued into his room, put on headphones, and popped *One Way Home* into the cassette deck. His thoughts drifted to something that had happened too soon to be called a memory, but eventually would be.

7

Sam couldn't wait to tell Stephanie what had happened. He had all he could do to wait for the late morning slow down to talk to her.

"I went for a walk with that girl from driver's ed," he said.

"Jessica, right?"

Sam nodded.

"Where did you meet up?"

"The library."

"The library again, too cute," she said.

Sam blushed.

Stephanie wanted to hear more. "What did you guys do?"

"We walked out to the radio towers, and then up to the playground at Riverton School."

"That sounds like fun. When are you hanging out again?"

"I don't know."

"What do you mean you don't know?"

"She is going to New York to meet her little brother for the first time," he said, the words making him feel older for some reason. "She might move there."

Stephanie looked through the windows to the small open space outside, where a few skateboarders were taking a break from doing tricks on the huge concrete planters. "Things get complicated sometimes," she said. "I hope whatever she decides is best for her."

Sam was hoping Stephanie would tell him that Jessica would stay. He was not yet at a point where he could be unconditionally empathetic. What he wanted mattered most in his mind. Crushes were one thing, but at least for Sam, they had never led to anything except distant admiration and hopes dashed. Now that he had made a connection with a real true person who happened to be a crush, she might be moving away. Just as he was starting to feel sorry for himself, he remembered Karla. The magic distance between them would soon be breeched for the second time that summer.

He went into his room after work and took out *Welcome to the Real World*, his favorite cassette. Before pressing play, he heard, "Hey Sam." The smiling face of his little brother entered the room they once had shared. "Did you hear the Kincades are coming up?"

Sam nodded. Brothers shared a knowing glance. Thing was, it was all innocent. There was no expectation beyond the excitement of out of state girls sleeping under the same roof as their lucky souls. "Guess we'll be sharing a room again," Sam said.

"Probably the living room."

"Probably."

Ben went out and Sam pressed play on his cassette deck. Cascading synths mixed with sharp guitar delay. Images of a music video appeared in his mind; there was Karla on the fishing boat, wearing his jacket until the scene faded into Jessica Song sitting next to him on the planks of the radio towers. The two memories commingled in synapses as arpeggios fell in quick succession.

The computer baseball season reached its peak that week. Hot with August was the dormered room. Highway cars whizzed by as the sun set wide behind. Sam wanted to tell the boys about Jessica and what the week had wrought, but thought not.

"The Sox aren't going anywhere," Cal said from the waterbed as he glanced through the latest *Sporting News*.

"It sucks," added Garrett.

Sam wanted to believe they'd pull it out somehow, he always wanted to believe, but there wasn't much happening besides stand out seasons from a couple stars. "Boggs is having a good year," he said. "He's getting so close to .400."

"He won't get there," Garrett argued.

"He could, he's hit .400 for the equivalent of a season before."

"But April to October is totally different."

That all was true, but it didn't hurt to hope. "He finally is becoming a complete player."

"His fielding's not there yet."

"It's getting better."

"He'll never win a Gold Glove. And even if he ever did, it won't help them win this year," Garrett argued.

"At least his cards are going up in value," Cal put in.

It had been the summer of *Hardball*, yes, but it also had been the summer of baseball card speculation. Disposable income from part time jobs had made pockets flush enough to purchase in bulk if so desired. Garrett was best at it, going straight for sure things like Bonds and Larkin. Sam liked to buy low and speculate on under the radar players in the hopes that his investments would one day pay off.

"McNamara should be fired," Garrett said. The Sox manager had become yet another famous scapegoat.

Cal didn't agree. "They went to the World Series last

year."

"But they blew it."

"Buckner blew it."

"It wasn't just Buckner. There was the wild pitch by Stanley, and Schiraldi was awful too."

"The responsibility ultimately falls on the manager," argued Garrett.

"How are those bonehead plays McNamara's fault?"

"He should have put Stapleton in for Buckner in the bottom of the 10th."

Cal was getting worked up. "He wanted Buckner on the field when they won!"

"And it cost them!"

Sam stepped in. "They had two outs and two strikes on like five batters in a row. It's a lot of peoples' fault."

"Can we stop talking about this please?" requested Garrett. "It's depressing me."

The sixth game of the 1986 World Series was a traumatic event in their lives. The drama of the Championship Series with Dave Henderson's late home run against the Angels had made it seem a team of destiny; and then to face the mighty Mets juggernaut, and have a two games to zero series lead, then three to two, and not be able to close it out haunted New England for nearly two decades. The boys fell silent, the *Hardball* game went on. It was the sixth inning and Sam was up 4-1.

It was Garrett who opened the next topic. "Have you seen Jessica Song?" he asked without moving his eyes from the screen.

Sam thought for a moment. He wasn't sure how to handle the question. Any mention of their afternoon together was sure to bring further probing. He decided to go for it anyway. "We hung out the other day," he ventured.

Garrett pushed up a grin. Sam was pretty sure he knew what his friend was thinking, but surprisingly, a non-affected, "What did you guys do?" came out.

Sam took a deep breath. "We walked out to the radio towers."

"Ooooh," Cal couldn't help but put in.

"Shut up!" Sam said, sure he had made a mistake telling them.

"Jeez, don't be so sensitive."

Garrett was feeling nostalgic. "Remember when we went down there that time?"

Cal smiled. "Remember when we tried to get the old scoreboard out of the mud?"

"It's still there!" Sam said.

"How did things end up with Jessica?" Garrett asked as he pitched an electronic strike.

"She's going away for a while."

"Why?"

Sam thought about what Stephanie had said. "Things

get complicated sometimes," he repeated.

Both boys laughed. "What's that supposed to mean?" asked Garrett.

Sam smiled, he had one over on them, finally. "Whatever you want it to."

The sun went down and soon Sam was returning home on his bike. Twilight was done, the night was young, and the heat of the day still filled the air with welcoming. Sam pedaled his bike along familiar streets, past telephone poles and under streetlights until he reached his driveway, where he looked toward the radio towers. It was completely dark now and Sam could see a few stars peaking out of the night sky. One was up near the radio beacon. He imagined being down there at night with Jessica and the moon shining down instead of the sun. They would turn their heads to the stars above, and maybe towards each other, reaching for their first kiss.

8

The Riverton courts were occupied by summer camps so the boys had to pedal through Morrill's Corner to play ball. They rode past St. Joeseph's and the glittering gold dome of the convent. Across the street was the sprawling grounds of Evergreen Cemetery, with its great tombs and tranquil duck ponds. Eventually, they reached Lincoln Middle School; its deep red bricks shining proudly in the sun. There were two basketball courts on the side of the building. The one furthest from them was occupied by a couple younger kids shooting around. Nearer to them, three classmates were playing one on one on one. Kevin Robichaud, Jessica's supposed crush, was there. He was not quite so dapper in gym shorts and a t-shirt, but still, he pulled it off.

"Hey Kevin, you guys want to play three on three?"

Garrett asked.

"Sure."

Boombox was blasting Run-D.M.C. as each group of friends became a team. Cal knocked down the make-it take-it, earning the boys from Riverton the ball. Defensive match-ups lined up by size. Garrett checked the ball in to the tall kid on the other team. Sam went right to the bottom of the key and tried to post up. Robichaud was a couple inches shorter, but he was strong and played good defense. Garrett bounced a pass to a cutting Cal, who laid it in, 1-0.

After checking the ball, Garrett tried the same thing. It was a bad pass. Robichaud intercepted it and cleared it at the top of the key. Sam put up a hand to defend, but his rival knocked down a jump shot. Before long, the boys from Riverton found themselves down by three.

"Play defense!" Garrett demanded of his teammates.

"Your guy scored too!" Cal shot back.

Robichaud tried again from outside, but missed. This time Sam gathered up the rebound and fired it to Garrett at the top of the key. His friend gave it right back and Sam hit an open jumper from the corner.

"Nice shot," Kevin said.

"Thanks," replied Garrett.

Maybe Robichaud wasn't so bad after all. It wasn't his fault Jessica had a crush on him. The game was a close one, but the home team won. They played one more, and this time the boys from Riverton came out ahead. Afternoon was in bloom as they rode home the same way they had come.

"You handled that well," Garrett said to Sam.

"What are you going to do? It's not Robichaud's fault that Jessica *had* a crush on him."

"Had?" Cal came back with.

Sam smiled and pedaled ahead.

Once back home, a fair amount of time was spent wondering if Jessica had returned from New York. He decided it was time to take a chance and call. The numbers were no easier to press than last time. The phone ringing on the other end was no less easier to take. He was wondering if the timing of the tones matched exactly on both ends when the call was answered.

"Hello?" asked Jessica's grandmother.

"Hi," Sam began with trepidation. "Is Jessica there?"

"No, she is out of town."

"Can you tell her Sam called?"

"Does she have your number?"

"I don't think so," he said before providing digits that if pressed would send a signal through wires to the phone before him.

"I'll leave it on her desk."

"Thank you."

All he could do now was wait. He was so new to this game, or whatever it was. It was not easy, that was for sure. Hopefully he would get some advice at the restaurant.

Stephanie asked if he had tried to call as soon as the morning rush subsided. "Yes," was the answer.

"What happened?"

"She hasn't come back from New York."

"From meeting her brother?"

Sam nodded.

Stephanie stared out at the little courtyard on the other side of the glass. There were a couple skateboarders out there, jumping up and sliding on the concrete planters. Things get complicated sometimes is what she had said before. He wondered what that meant. The waitress's contemplative eyes turned into a smile. Steve was coming up the walk. He entered the restaurant and took a seat at the counter. "How's your shift going?" he asked his girlfriend.

"Great, just hanging with my work boyfriend," she said, putting her arm around Sam's shoulder.

Steve smiled. "Guess I have some competition."

And with that, Stephanie was off to clear the corner table, where a party was leaving.

"How's the guitar playing going?" Steve asked the bus boy.

Sam wished he could say it was going great, but he had not picked it up in a while. "I think about playing a lot," he said.

"Why don't you?"

Sam was ashamed to say. "It's not in tune."

"That's an easy fix."

"For you maybe."

Steve chuckled. "Just get a tuner. Come to think of it, I may have an extra one kicking around somewhere. If I can find it, it's yours."

"Thanks!"

Stephanie came back around. "You guys talking shop?"

"You know how we musicians are," Steve said.

Stephanie's rolling eyes told Sam she did. She changed the topic. "Sam might have found himself a girlfriend," she said.

"Good looking kid like Sam, I'm sure he has," Steve said.

"They walked down to the radio towers together. Doesn't that sound romantic?"

Steve smiled. "Sounds like the start of something to me."

"We never do stuff like that," Stephanie said.

Steve laughed. "You want me to take you down to the radio towers?"

"Not that necessarily, but something spontaneous once in a while would be nice."

"I'll try to do better."

"That's all I ask."

It was settled and Sam walked over to set up the corner table Stephanie had just cleared. He thought about the guitar sitting in the box in his closet. How he wished he could make the strings sing. Sam thought about the radio towers and the time he had spent with Jessica.

The very same towers beckoned that afternoon. Sam walked through the path to Lane Avenue, then down the dusty dirt road extension, where the boys used to ride bikes. Plastic foam headphones went over Sam's ears. The new Bryan Adams tape was in the deck. It seemed all the music artists he liked had gone serious, Adams included, especially on the first side of *Into the Fire*. The title track came on with pinging synths, big drums, and guitars that sounded like they were being played from a mountaintop. It was epic, no doubt. Beats per minute matched his step until fade out. The opening bass drop to 'Victim of Love' made Sam wonder if that's what he was. There was Jessica, not that far away, not that long ago. Sam imagined her holding her little brother and never wanting to leave. Why would she? She could read him books and sing him radio songs and all the other things he imagined that cool big sisters did. By the time he reached the end of the dirt road, Sam felt sad. The windowless white house was unattended as always. Up ahead were the three looming radio towers. Two had square bases that tapered toward the top. Wires from one to another connected them together in a unity of transmission. He could only imagine the electrical languages they spoke. The boy climbed the planks and began toward the towers.

Side one ended. As he took out the cassette to flip it over, he heard someone yelling, "Hey kid! Kid! Get down from there!"

Sam turned to see a paunchy middle-aged man emerging from a white Econoline van. The man was waving both hands above his head. "You're trespassing! Didn't you see the sign?"

Sam had seen it out of the corner of his eye, but shook his head anyway. He began down the ladder with a little worry.

In work overalls and a painter's cap, the man didn't look very intimidating. His hands remained on hips until the boy reached him.

"Sorry," Sam said.

The man looked stern. He wagged a plump finger toward the towers. "This is all the property of the station."

"What station?"

The guy sort of grinned. Evidently, this wasn't the response his authority usually inspired. "WPOR," he said.

"I don't like country music."

"Me neither," the man admitted with a chuckle. "You can't be out here though. You're lucky it was me and not the cops, they probably would have given you a bit of a hassle."

"Sorry," Sam said again. He had an urge to explain to the man how he and Jessica had walked out on the planks, and about how she had yet to return his call, but he did not.

The man lifted his hat to reveal a balding head. "No worries kid, I did the same kind of things when I was your age," he said before trying to look stern again. He was having a hard time of it. "Just don't let me catch you out there again," he said.

"You won't," Sam replied without knowing whether he was telling the truth. He turned and began walking away.

Just as he was about to start side two, the man called out, "Hey kid, what are you listening to?"

Sam turned. "Bryan Adams."

The guy pretended to play guitar and belted out the chorus of 'Summer of '69'. Sam chuckled as he turned back around and pressed play. He made his way back the way he came. Nobody was home. He stared at the phone and thought about pressing the numbers that would connect him to Jessica, but what if she wasn't there? He decided it best not to call that afternoon. Into his room he went. The closet door was open and there amongst his baseball cards was the cardboard box that held his guitar. He took it out and sat on his bed. E minor he remembered, and there was a partial G. Those were the go-tos. Out of tune strings sounded nothing like the clean tone of the Bob Clearmountain mixed album he had been listening to earlier. It seemed so far away. After a minute or two of ragged strumming, he put the guitar back in its case and closed the closet door.

9

The sun was blaring loud one afternoon when the boys decided to ride into town. They followed Forest Avenue through Woodford's, then down along Back Cove. Sam looked over at the city, his city. Two hills rose; Munjoy to the East, Bramhall, not quite so dramatic, to the West. The boys passed the Shop n' Save on the boulevard and went up the hill into the heart of the peninsula. Sam shifted to his lowest gear to make it. Garrett was up ahead of him. Cal got caught at a light on Cumberland, but managed to catch up pretty quickly. They pedaled down Congress until Monument Square, there they dismounted in a triangle facing one another.

"What do you think?" Sam asked.

"Let's lock our bikes here and walk," Garrett suggested. "Where do you guys want to go?"

"Bad Habits," Sam said.

"Levinsky's," Cal put in.

It wasn't the mall, but that was a good thing on such a beautiful day. They walked toward Temple Street, and the Nickelodeon, where the three had seen *E.T.* years before. They talked Sox as they walked. Nearly ten games below .500 this late in the season meant it was time to admit there was too much ground to make up.

Garrett blamed his favorite scapegoat, "McNamara has got to go, there's too much talent for them to be so dull."

"But he led them to the World Series," Cal argued once again.

The argument had no end. Yeah, McNamara made some questionable decisions, but players failed to execute at crucial moments; Stanley, Gedman, Schiraldi, and of course, Buckner. Poor Bill Buckner got most of the blame. The man was the soul of the team with 116 RBI, and almost 20 stolen bases on knees that were shot. One ball went through the guy's legs at the exact wrong moment, and the hopes and dreams of all New England came crashing down on his shoulders. It was a fate he did not deserve. There was still a game seven, Oil Can Boyd was pitching and they were up 3-0 early, but it was not to be.

"What do *you* think Sam?" Cal asked, hoping to swing the balance against Garrett.

"They definitely aren't going anywhere this year," he

admitted.

That was the last word, they were almost at Bad Habits anyway. It wasn't much of a record store anymore. Cassettes, stacked high in theft-proof plastic cases, had pretty much taken over. Compact discs were housed in a growing central space. Records were up in the back, stacked in a terraced display case. The format had become an outcast, dismissed as obsolete. Sam only had a couple local LPs by the Boyz and the Kopterz, but he had a bunch of 45s. The sound was powerful, but cassettes sounded good too, and they were portable. He could put them in his walkman and listen to the latest album by Journey as he rode his bike. The 'J' section of cassettes happened to be before him. There it was. He pulled *Raised on Radio* out of the rack, looked at the cover, and smiled. Radio towers were connected by a sort of lightning electricity emanating from its beacons. It reminded him of the towers down the dirt road. The sleek Art Deco station house on the cover though, bore little resemblance to the plain white one he knew.

"Is *Diver Down* any good?" he heard Cal ask.

Garrett was an expert on all things Van Halen. "It's no *1984*," was the verdict.

Sam found Mr. Mister, his favorite band. The new album was coming out, but not quite yet.

"Sam," he heard Cal call. "You ready?"

The three friends stepped out onto Exchange Street

and passed Post Office Park with its mix of homeless and workers sitting outside for lunch. There were also city kids hanging about, Portland High School students, most likely. Sam noticed another group, one of teenage bohemians, closer to Market Street.

"Sam," Garrett said, "it's your girlfriend."

Sam looked closer at the group of skaters and punks. Kat's cheshire smile was coming toward him. His pals moved away to leave boy and girl alone.

Summer didn't change Kat's style of dancer flats and genie pants one bit. "Wow, Sam Rinaldo venturing downtown," she said. "What brings you fellows out?"

"Looking for music and going to Levinsky's."

"Sounds about right."

Sam didn't mind how she gave him heck sometimes. It kept him off balance in a good way. "What about you?"

"Oh, you know, took the bus downtown to meet up with friends."

He may have been talking to Kat, but Sam was thinking of Jessica. He wondered if the two kept in touch over the summer. Probably not. Still, he was dying to find out if Jessica was back from New York. Sam though, remained silent.

"Hey Kat, we're going to the beach," a husky female voice called. The whole lot of nonconformists started moving in that direction.

Kat sighed. "I hate the beach," she said to Sam. "Oh well, got to go, but I can't wait to tell you about drama camp, it was so awesome," she said, cupping her hands together. "I'll see you soon enough."

"Yeah, see ya," he said. He watched her walk away and thought about how Jessica was right, Kat was very much herself. He wondered how much like himself he was, and as he returned to his friends, he wondered the same about them.

"She's so weird," Cal said.

"She's definitely herself," Sam replied, feeling wise saying it.

Garrett grinned. "We better get out of here before Sam develops a crush on Kat too."

They walked to Congress Street, past city hall until they reached Levinsky's. It was the *chic* spot for style in the city. For such a popular destination, the well-kept triple decker at the foot of Munjoy Hill couldn't have been more unassuming.

They moved past cash register lines of school shopping kids and parents to the room where walls were filled with footwear: Reebok, Nike, Adidas. Boat shoes were in for sure. Sam thought he should ask his mother for some. On to the clothes they went. Sam stopped to look at the bin of folded pinstriped Oxford shirts wrapped in plastic. Not far were racks of pastel surfing t-shirts, surely popular everywhere else before Maine.

Back past the registers they went, where people were still packed together awaiting checkout.

Garrett's voice suddenly rose above the din. "Sam," he said with some urgency, "it's Jessica."

Garrett pointed his finger toward the check out. Sam's eyes followed its direction. The girl had heard and turned her eyes down toward things the cashier was ringing up. To Sam, Jessica looked even prettier than the day they walked to the radio towers. The graying woman that stood behind her had to be her grandmother. With them was a pretty, younger woman, most likely Jessica's mother. Sam froze. He mustered a small wave that did not make it past his shoulder. The inertia of the boys pushed him out the door and back onto Congress Street just as Jessica was reciprocating the wave.

Anger rose inside of Sam. He pushed Garrett with some intent. "You're a jerk," he said.

Garrett laughed. "What?"

"She heard you."

"So?"

"So?" returned Sam. "You embarrassed her, and me."

"Would you rather I didn't tell you?"

Deep breaths calmed Sam. There was nothing for it. What happened had happened. No more was said as they walked back to their bikes. Going down Forest Avenue was a lot easier than coming up. Hair blew back as Back Cove came into view. There was no stoplight to slow them until they reached the boulevard. The tide was high with turquoise water reflecting glistening sunshine.

10

The restaurant was crazy on Saturday morning. Sam was running all over the place, clearing tables and bringing dishes to Luis in the kitchen. Cooks were barking orders at one another and tickets were flying everywhere. It was about 9:30 when he looked up and saw Jessica and her grandmother getting into a booth he had just cleared and set. Instinct sent him right back into the kitchen. Luis looked up at him, expecting more dishes. Sam's face was red and his heart was beating fast. There was the embarrassment at Levinsky's, and before that, the phone call that was never returned. What other calamity could possibly await? He could only imagine.

"You okay?" a voice asked him.

Sam looked at Luis's pockmarked face and fluffy afro under that blue and white mesh cap. The boy wondered if

Luis ever felt as he did now. If so, it would have likely been in Cuba, long ago. Sam sometimes wondered what circumstances led Luis to become a dishwasher in this corner of the world.

"Yeah, I'm okay, thank you," Sam said before gaining courage and marching back into the dining room. There was Jessica at the table by the window. Stephanie was at the coffee maker, loading a new filter into its place. He wanted to tell her, but the big round table in the corner needed to be cleared. Sam carried over the gray plastic tub and got to work. Dishes were first, empty but for pooled syrup, or yolks strewn by toast. White coffee mugs were next into the tub. Water and soda from hard plastic glasses was consolidated into one, inside of which went silverware, tines down. Used cream and sugar packets were wrapped in placemats before being wedged into the organized mess. As he was heading back for the rag bucket and new place settings, he turned and caught sight of Jessica. The sunlight shined through the window and on eyes that caught his. Sam was still a bit hurt she hadn't returned his call. He pursed his lips and nodded, she did the same.

"Sam, table three needs your magic touch," said Eleanor. He looked over; sure enough, another table needed clearing and he hadn't even wiped down the one in front of him. Back he went to the counter with the busing tray. There was the rag bucket, thankfully filled with warm soapy water and clean rags. Sam raced back over to the corner table and wiped it down. Eleanor was right behind him with place settings. He had another table to clear. There was a line waiting out through the glass doors and into the gorgeous morning.

The busing tray was soon filled again. Luis would hate to see this. Eleanor approached just as he was about to push open the swinging kitchen door. "Luis needs your help," she said.

Oh great, thought Sam. This had happened before, but not when Jessica was sitting in the dining room. Now, he would be stuck in the steaming dishwashing station for who knows how long.

Sam set the tub down and Luis's eyes went big. "I'm here to help," the boy said.

Luis made the sign of the cross and looked toward heaven.

Sam knew the routine well enough. Luis sprayed loose food from the dishes into the hungry disposal before handing them to Sam, who placed them on wide plastic trays to go into the dishwasher.

Stephanie brought in another full busing tub. "Fun times," she said to Sam before looking over at Luis. "You okay?" she asked him.

The latter nodded. Everything was okay.

Once clean cups and silverware had cooled enough,

Sam brought the tray into the dining room and started unloading mugs onto paper towels on the counter. Jessica and her grandmother were getting up to leave. If he was doing his usual work, it would be him clearing that very table. Eleanor though, was on it. From his spot near the coffee machine, all Sam could do was wave. There was reciprocity. Jessica's grandmother looked toward him and managed a grin before pulling her purse over her shoulder. Sam watched as they stepped into summer.

"Cups don't stack themselves," Stephanie kindly jested.

"Jessica just left."

"The girl by the window?"

"Yes."

Stephanie smiled. "She's pretty."

"But I couldn't talk to her because it was so busy."

"Does she know you work here?"

"I don't know."

"You'll just have to call her again."

That's what he was afraid of, anxiously counting off long rings. Would she answer? Was she off again to her mother and little brother in New York?

The worst of the rush was definitely over. The boy went back into the kitchen. Luis was officially caught up. "Thank you Sam," he said.

It wasn't Luis's fault that Sam didn't get to talk to Jessica. "You're welcome."

The place was practically empty by the time the late morning lull came around. Luis felt comfortable enough to poke his head out for a glass of Pepsi. Sal and the other cook were having a smoke with the delivery guy.

Stephanie was clearing off a recently abandoned table. Sam went over to her. "I can get this for you."

She looked at him like an older sister. "Poor Sam, you've had a rough day. Tell you what, I'll get this, you take a break."

He had started walking back toward the soda machine to pour himself a Pepsi when Stephanie called to him. "Did you ever find out how things worked out for Jessica?" she asked, motioning toward the table by the window.

Sam shook his head.

"You trying to steal my girlfriend?" asked a familiar voice. Sam looked up to see Steve's smiling face. "How's your guitar playing?" he asked his reluctant protege.

Sam shrugged. "Not so good."

Steve reached out a hand to Sam. In it was the tuner he had promised. "It probably needs batteries."

"Thanks!"

Stephanie looked at her boyfriend with soft eyes. "I guess maybe you can be a nice guy sometimes," she said.

"I have my moments," Steve replied before turning his attention back to Sam. "No more excuses about why you're not playing," he said before shifting gears. "While I'm thinking of it, the band is playing at the Riverton Grange Hall next Saturday night. It's an all ages show. I can get you in free if you want."

Stephanie touched Sam's shoulder. "You could bring Jessica," she said excitedly.

He remembered something. Karla Kincade and her family were going to be visiting. "That girl from Connecticut will be up with her family," he said.

"Bring the girl from Connecticut then."

Sam smiled. Images of he and Karla dancing to a guitar pop tune took away much of the disappointment of not talking to Jessica.

After riding home from work, he pushed his bike up the driveway and into the backyard. His mother was in the kitchen. Cookies were cooling on the counter.

"Ma," he began, "do you remember me telling you Stephanie's boyfriend plays in a band?"

A cautious, "Yes," came from her.

Sam was nervous. He could think of few things he wanted more at that moment than to take Karla to the show. "Well, his band is playing at the Grange Hall next Saturday and I was thinking maybe me and Karla could go."

Sam's mother liked Stephanie, was thankful for her even. She was a good enough parent to see the confidence the young woman gave her son. "What kind of music is it?"

she asked.

"Rock music."

"Heavy metal?"

Sam laughed. He remembered something Stephanie once told him. "No Mom, kind of like REM."

"Rapid eye movement?"

Sam couldn't help but chuckle. "It's a band."

His mother thought for a few seconds. "I guess it's fine with me. We'll have to ask Gretchen if it's okay for Karla to go. I don't want you kids walking down there at night, your father will drop you off and pick you up."

Fine by Sam. He went into his room and turned on the stereo. There was only one thing he wanted to hear. Out from his walkman came the cassette. It was placed into one of his stereo decks. Headphones resting on the closed turntable went over his ears and soon the sounds of 'Karla With a K' were dancing around his head.

11

The boys decided to ride their bikes down to the card shop on Warren Avenue. Wasn't long before they reached the large two-story white paneled building. RBI Sports Cards was tucked into a corner, facing away from the road. Tony, the owner, had a regular adult job and a family. He opened two late afternoons a week, and on Saturdays. Tony didn't make much off these three, but understood the value of returning customers. "What brings you fellas out this way?" he asked upon their entrance.

Sam cut to the quick. He wanted bulk. "Do you have any Topps cello cases?"

Tony pointed to the floor at the end of the glass display case he was standing behind. "Just got a shipment in yesterday."

Sam looked down at the unopened green, blue, and

white boxes neatly stacked one on top of the other. How he wished he could possess them all. Inside each box was 36 packs containing 24 cards each. That was 864 cards. He imagined spending a rainy afternoon sorting through them while listening to his favorite tunes.

"How much?" asked Sam.

"Fourteen bucks."

It was a little more than Sam made in tips that morning. Still, the temptation was too great. He emptied his wallet of the fourteen one dollar bills it contained.

"How are you going to get that home?" asked Garrett.

"Carry it on my bike."

"Better hope you don't drop it."

Tony jumped in, anxious for a sale, "You can pick it up later if you want."

Sam turned to Garrett. "I'll be fine."

That settled it.

"Anything else I can do you guys for?" asked Tony.

"You got any McGwire Olympic cards?" Garrett inquired.

"Only in sets," Tony replied ruefully.

"How much are the sets?"

"Forty."

Garrett grimaced.

"It's a fair price."

Garrett knew it was, but forty dollars was a lot to pay

for a set filled with commons he had multiples of at home. Conversation turned to the Red Sox as it usually did.

"They should have called up Sam Horn sooner," Garrett put forth, yet again beating the drum for immediate change.

"Maybe," countered Tony, "we'll see if he can hit the curveball."

"What do you think the problem is this year?" Sam asked the elder.

Tony looked at the youths. "Nineteen eighty-six," he said.

That was the last word. They all knew it to be true. But what could be done? Boggs and Clemens were unquestionably superstars, Greenwell was coming into his own. The talent was there, but ghosts hovered over Fenway Park, ghosts from long ago brought into the here and now.

The three boys stepped into bright sunshine and thick, humid air. Sam climbed onto his bike with the Topps cello case under his arm. He pushed off on the asphalt and soon was on the go.

Cal was already riding shotgun when Garrett picked up Sam that early evening. The back seat was the only option. Soon they were moving down Route One through Scarborough, where only road interrupts marshes almost as far as the eye can see. FM 103 was playing Huey Lewis and the News in honor of that night's show at The Ballpark at Old Orchard Beach. Marshes ended and old farm buildings mixed with new strip malls. Garrett took a left on to 98 at the Cascades. The giant flea market was closed for the day and the chocolate brown cottages across the street had no vacancies, as was usually the case in summer. Pine Point was next with its seafood places and flood of seagulls on the wing.

"Let's drive down to the strip," suggested Sam.

Garrett shook his head. "We got to get to the show," he answered like a parent.

"I agree with Garrett," Cal said.

"Come on. There's plenty of time," argued Sam.

To Sam, the strip of Old Orchard Beach was America. Old hotels with mid-century neon signs lit the night like many colored starlight. Grand Street was tamer when the sun was out, but still pretty exciting. There was Palace Playland with the Galaxi roller coaster and the pirate ship swinging high. Quebecois poured in every summer. "*Je me sovereign*," their license plates read. Sam could picture them walking to and fro, emerging from beach hotels with names like Waves, Driftwood, and The Crest. Many times he had seen it all from the backseat of his parents' car. If the weather was nice, the family would park and walk around.

Garrett looked up into the rearview mirror at Sam. "The strip will take too long. I'm nervous about parking at the Ballpark, it's probably pretty backed up," he said in a voice that implied he might have complied with the request if circumstances were different.

"There will be a lot of girls down there," suggested Sam.

Garrett laughed. "Okay playboy, what would you do about it?"

Cal thought that was funny.

Sam leaned back in his seat as 'Heart and Soul' blasted on tinny speakers. What would he do? What could he do now but sit in the backseat on his way to the show?

Garrett was right, the line to get into the stadium was long. Rectangular cars moved at a snail's pace. Vendors had set up booths in the shoulder of the road, selling t-shirts, posters, and other merchandise. He cringed when he thought of the heck Kat would give him if she saw him in a Huey Lewis t-shirt. The singer was popular, but cool he was not. He even had a huge hit song in which he bragged about that fact. This was why he appealed to such a wide variety of people, like the light metal heads that were Sam's friends.

Cars eventually moved enough to allow them entrance into the huge parking lot, where orange vested attendants guided them to a spot. The three boys followed rivulets of people until they reached the gate. Tickets were taken and torn before they moved through turnstiles and into the open concourse with people moving everywhere. Kids their own age were scattered amongst beer-bellied middle-aged men in tank tops walking with their wives. Maine Guides games drew a good crowd, but this was on another level. Lines were long at the wooden concession stands. The scent of fried dough filled the concourse ballplayers had to walk through to get to the field. The three boys had collected countless autographs from these AAA players, most of whom were going nowhere except maybe a cup of coffee in the big leagues. Still, they were like idols to adolescents for whom baseball formed a sort of religion.

Up concrete steps they marched until the holy diamond stretched before them. Trees waved behind the fence. Home run distances were painted near the foul poles. The outfield was filled with people, and there in center field was the stage. Timing was just about perfect. Bonnie Hays and her band came out pretty much right away. It was pleasant enough pop music most of the crowd ignored.

Cal turned to them when her set finished. "You guys want to go for a walk?"

"Yeah," Garrett replied, "I want to get a t-shirt."

Back down into the concourse they wandered. It was an older crowd than the Bryan Adams show, for sure. A lot of children were even with their parents. He saw girls he assumed were from places like Scarborough and Saco, and who knows where else; Bridgton, Buxton, maybe even further afield.

"There are so many people here," Cal said.

Garrett nodded. "Way more than any Guides game I've ever been to, even against Pawtucket."

Pawtucket was the Red Sox farm team and their games always sold out.

They waved at some kids from school over by the fried dough vendor.

"Here are the t-shirts," Garrett said.

"You gonna get one Sam?" Cal asked.

"Nah," he demurred.

Sam couldn't tell them the biggest reason he didn't want to get a shirt was because Kat would make fun of him. She would be gentle, but would tell him in no uncertain terms how she felt about Huey Lewis and the News.

The three of them were soon back in their seats to watch roadies setting up gear. "Check, check, check," one would say into a microphone, then another; a different guy would strum a guitar. Sam watched with rapt attention. It was a knowable mystery, but yet unknowable, in many ways similar to the game played on the field before them.

The band came out and started playing 'Jacob's Ladder' and soon as he was supposed to, Huey Lewis ran up to the microphone and started singing. The crowd went wild. The set was hit packed and crowd pleasing, but about an hour into the show, the sky darkened and rain came pouring down. The band kept playing and the crowd that didn't seek shelter embraced the downpour.

"It's raining like hell, but do we care?" asked Huey Lewis.

The crowd roared, "No!"

Hit after hit kept coming and soon enough the rain stopped and the last glimpses of the setting sun were visible through the clouds. "We've been told there are over sixteen thousand people here," the singer said between songs. The crowd roared. "We've also been told this might be the largest crowd ever assembled in Maine." The crowd roared louder. "Thank you Maine!" he shouted as the band launched into 'Back in Time' and the crowd went wild, yet again.

When the song ended, the band put down their instruments and made their way off the stage. The crowd wasn't having any of it, and soon the band returned. Lewis walked up to the microphone, "We've got official word that this is the largest crowd ever assembled in Maine. Thank you!"

Spotlights lit the night and panned down on the sixteen thousand plus souls gathered there. Three about-to-be juniors let go their inhibitions and started dancing to the pop rock music. They were still wet from the rain, but it mattered not one bit.

Sam looked down toward the field and could not believe his eyes. There, in the section below, was Kat, dancing joyously as he. The fact that she was at the show was shocking enough, but to see her dancing was too much. Every so often Kat would high five an older woman, who had to be her mom.

The show ended with a long ovation as the band stood together bowing and waving from the stage. Lights came on and people began to make their way out of the small stadium and into the parking lot. It took the boys a while to find the powder blue Escort. Garrett turned the ignition and Huey Lewis came on the radio.

"That was the best show," Cal said.

All three agreed, music had set them free. The fact that it had been created by a self-proclaimed square mattered not one bit. They rhapsodized about what they had witnessed while waiting in the long line of cars leaving the dirt parking lot.

Eventually they reached the light across from the fire station and made their way into the night. It was too late to go to the strip now, but Sam couldn't help but wish to go where the action is.

12

The anticipation of Karla's arrival made Sam both excited and anxious. It was perhaps the greatest visitation he had yet known. Their time together earlier in the summer had promised everything, yet nothing. If she accompanied him to the Grange Hall for the show, it would be kind of like a date. That excited him, but he also worried that she was out of his league. She was so pretty and had that certain *savoir faire* of someone growing up a train ride away from New York City.

It was not only seeing Karla that gave his mind pause. School would be starting directly after the holiday. It wasn't as bad as it sounded; he would see all kinds of friends, and hopefully, Jessica. The long grind of the school year is what he dreaded; the getting up early and not being able to do what he wanted, when he wanted.

There was business to attend to before that. Mr. Mister's new album was finally out. The two years since the last one seemed an eternity. Portland had just got MTV when 'Broken Wings' hit with its stark black and white desert scenes. Its washes of synth and guitar had entranced Sam. He talked Garrett into driving out to the mall so he could see if any of the stores had it. The parking lot was packed. School shopping was in full effect mode and had forced them to park far away from their normal spot. Over the hot asphalt they trudged to their preferred entrance at the corner by JC Penney, between Tape World and Record Town. Both were basically tape stores now. Sam walked up to the wall of cassettes at the M's and looked at the titles. He found *Welcome to the Real World*, and even the relatively rare first album, *I Wear the Face*, both of which he had; the new one however, was nowhere to be found.

Behind the counter stood the short, blond mulletted kid with the pencil mustache. "Can I help you?" he asked.

"Do you guys have the new Mr. Mister tape?"

The guy smirked. "If it isn't in the rack, we don't have it. Did you check the other store?"

Sam crossed over to Record Town, no luck.

He found Garrett and Cal easy enough, they were going through the AC/DC catalog, discussing the merits of each release.

"They don't have it," Sam informed them.

"I don't blame them," Garrett said, sharp.

Into the masses they marched, past mothers carrying bags alongside their mostly adolescent children. He recognized some of the kids from school, many more he did not. They ran into some guys they knew; one had bought a car over the summer, the other had worked a lot. Sam didn't say much, his eyes were focused on Musicland across the sunny center plaza of the mall.

"I'm going to head over there," Sam said.

Nobody responded. He walked away imagining they were dissing his taste in music. Sam didn't care.

The skylight that lit the center plaza of the mall shined upon steps leading down to a sunken space with benches. Above were windows open to the true blue late summer sky. Sam continued on, weaving through people passing perpendicular to him. Two girls in jean shorts and pastel tank tops passed just before he reached the store's entrance. Sam gave them the eye and the one closest to him smiled.

Inside Musicland, he passed the rack of 45s he had looked through many times. A little ways down, on the left, was the wall of cassettes. He continued on until he reached the shelf he was looking for. There it was. Sam grabbed his prize. It was going to cost him $10.99 plus tax. The diminutive cover was off white with something between a picture and a painting. There was a time worn road, and in the distance, one single tree. *Go On...* was the title of the album. Sam was pretty sure it all represented something, but he had no idea what. One thing he did know though, Mr. Mister had gone serious like The Hooters and Bryan Adams before them. He guessed it was a good thing without knowing why. Sam brought the cassette to the register. There was a bit of a line. He was reading the names of the song titles when he noticed the girls in tank tops standing behind him. His heart started beating faster. Both of them were tan, but one, more so. "What are you buying?" she asked.

Sam thought her friend was prettier at first glance, but the more he looked at the girl speaking to him, the more he changed his mind; she had long corkscrew hair and smiling eyes. Sam was kind of embarrassed at his purchase, but there was nothing for it. "The new Mr. Mister album," he said.

The girl smiled. "I like them."

"My friends don't," complained Sam.

The girl pointed up to the cashier waiting for him to hand over his purchase. The young woman lifted the key attached to the counter and unlocked the cassette, setting the tape free from its hard plastic prison and into a small white bag. "Eleven fifty-four," she said.

Sam took out his wallet and gave her two fives and two ones he had worked so hard to earn.

"Forty-six cents is your change," said the woman behind the counter.

Sam took the change and put it into his pocket. He took the bag in his hand and stepped aside so the girls could approach the register.

"Enjoy your tape," the one he had been talking to said.

"Thanks," smiled Sam.

Back into the masses he stepped with mind riding high from the interaction. Garrett and Cal were saying goodbye to school mates when he reached them. Together they checked out the usual stores: American Eagle, Walden's, and Prints Plus for posters they looked at, but never bought.

FM 103 soundtracked the way home. The DJ said something about summer coming to an end. Hard to believe it was true. 'La Isla Bonita' came on the stereo. It was a song that sounded like summer, with a hook sweet as ice cream. Sam thought about mentioning that Karla was coming up. It was very possible, in fact, that she would accompany him to a rock show at the Grange Hall. Problem with that was the last thing in the world he wanted was them there with he and Karla. Garrett and Cal would embarrass him, no doubt. He found something else to say instead.

"I talked to this girl in line at Musicland," he announced from the backseat.

"Did she laugh at what you bought?" Garrett asked into the rearview mirror.

"No, she actually said she liked Mr. Mister," Sam said, trying to prove a point.

"She was probably just trying to make you feel better."

It was no use. Sam wondered if liking Mr. Mister was part of what made up who he was and wondered whether it was a good thing or not.

First thing Sam did when he got home was pop in the cassette for which he had waited so long. Sure enough, Mr. Mister had gone serious too, but in this case, not for the better. *Billboard* had given the album a good review, but to Sam, their ambition to be taken seriously left behind the hooks.

His father's footsteps sounded in the hallway. "Sam," he said. "I need you to mow the lawn."

It was not what the son wanted to do, but there was little choice in the matter. Sam grabbed the new cassette and put it in his walkman, hoping to loosen ear worms as yet undiscovered.

13

Sam awaited the arrival of Karla with nervous energy. It led him to his bike. He first thought to ride down by Jessica's house, maybe she would be out and he would be able to talk to her. Courage failed him though and instead he rode in the opposite direction down 302, towards Westbrook. Def Leppard was in his walkman, and as sophomore summer came to a close, the band was everywhere. Past Papa's Place he wheeled. It was where he and the boys played Donkey Kong on Sunday mornings of sixth grade. Further on he went, under the overpass, then past Tortilla Flats. Riverton Park was next on the left. People called it the project. He had never been inside, but often wondered what it was like. A few of his elementary classmates who grew up there were no longer in school. On he went until Riverside, where he took a right. There, he stopped at the field where his baseball dreams began.

Three kids younger than him were playing baseball: one was hitting, one pitching, one in left field. Sam stopped to watch. The kid that was hitting was pretty good, dropping it near the outfield fence almost every single time. He remembered when he used to play on that very field and imagined himself being good enough to go all the way.

"Hey kid," came a voice from home plate. "You want to play?"

Sam smiled. "No, thanks anyway," he said.

His counterpart nodded in acknowledgement and got back to the game.

Sam could go back home, or up towards the Riverside Golf Course, but something in the back of his mind came to the fore. He remembered the stone pillars just a little further down Forest Avenue.

Trapezoid cars were piled up at the light, Sam coasted slowly down the slim shoulder of Route 302, which eventually led into the mountains of New Hampshire and Vermont. Overgrown vegetation obscured the stone pillars that were a crumbling reminder of a bygone day, when they served as an entrance to Riverton Trolley Park. Sam's father had told him about the roller coaster and casino that once entertained passengers waiting for connecting trains. Travelers would take the inter-urban from Morrill's Corner to spend carefree hours by the riverside.

He pushed his bike through the lightly worn trail. There, to his left, the green river slowly wound its way. He brought his bike down close to the nearly still water and rested it against a tree. A collapsed trunk reached into the water. Sam edged his way up on it. The river wasn't very wide, but on the other bank was Westbrook. Birds above sang as they winged to destinations known only to them. Headphones went over ears and 'Hysteria' filled aural space with watery guitar lines. His heart beat as his mind drifted to the arrival of Karla.

Wasn't long before it happened. He was in the living room watching MTV with Ben. Neither brother was saying much, both were anxious in their own way. 'With or Without You' filled the twenty-six inch screen with grainy black and white. Their parents went out to greet the guests. Sam looked down at Ben. The boys shared a knowing, nervous grin.

"The moment of reckoning," said the younger brother.

Sam wondered how his little brother came up with such things. "Yeah," he said.

"Should we go out?"

"I suppose we should."

Sam put down the cable box and turned off the television. Being the oldest, he led the way. Radio towers stood in the distance, blinking slow incessant rhythms. A quick thought of Jessica arose only to be pushed down by the here and now. Parents hugged one another. Sam didn't see Karla and started to get worried until she emerged after her little sister.

Gretchen made her way over to him for a hug. "The summer has done you well," she said. Sam blushed, he wondered if her daughter felt the same.

The four kids then retreated to the backyard, where the garden was red with tomatoes.

Sam turned to Karla. "Have you heard the new Def Leppard album?" he asked.

"I don't like pop metal, or any other type of metal for that matter," was the curt reply.

It was not the start he had imagined. Sam took a deep breath and listened as his little brother and Tina carried on like old friends.

He went for gold right away. "This band is playing at the Grange Hall tomorrow night. Do you think your parents would let you go?"

"What kind of music do they play?"

"They're kind of like REM. I think you'd like them," Sam said, even though he himself had never heard them.

"What are they called?"

"The Next Wave."

Karla nodded, but that was all. Sam worried he had handled the situation poorly, that he should have waited to ask. Now it was all out there, for better or worse.

Families soon piled into their own cars and the visitors followed down through Woodford's Corner, to the boulevard, then the peninsula. Sam looked out the window. Thoughts on how to rectify the situation bounced through his head. He decided to remain quiet for the time being. They went to the Village, an Italian restaurant long woven into the fabric of the city. There was a wait. Once they were seated, families each took a side of the booth. Kids faced each other on the end. Ben and Tina were talking about shows on Nickelodeon with some intensity.

Sam's silent act wasn't getting the response from Karla that he had hoped. Finally, Gretchen looked at her eldest daughter. "Would you quit your moping?"

Karla said nothing, now embarrassed that her mother had called her out in front of everybody.

Gretchen looked around the table. "Karla didn't want to come because one of her friends is having a party tomorrow night."

"Everyone is going to be there," the daughter said in her defense.

"You can't go to every party, my dear," replied her mother.

Karla looked to be on the verge of tears. Sam felt sorry for her, but more sorry for himself. This was not turning out how he had imagined at all. He tried to think of a song that captured how he was feeling, the bass drop beginning of 'Victim of Love' echoed in his head.

"Try and make the best out of being here," Gretchen pleaded gently.

'Make the best out of being here,' Sam repeated in his head. Not exactly what he imagined Gretchen saying to her daughter in front of him. Maybe it could be a lyric in a song. Whatever it was, it did not change the affect of the teenage girl sitting across from him in a large booth at his favorite restaurant. Fresh Botto's bread and baked manicotti had never tasted so bitter.

Dinner done, they rode up to the Promenade at the tip of Munjoy Hill. They looked out over the islands of Casco Bay. Peaks was there, seemingly so close, and then there was Great and Little Diamond. Closer still, Fort Gorges rose up out of tranquil waves. Ben and Tina followed their fathers to go climb the cannons. The mothers and two eldest stood observing the ocean scene.

Night was beginning its long descent upon the bay. Lights of ships blinked in the distance like beacons on radio towers. Karla went and sat by herself on a bench. Sam decided to make his way over. He could relate to being dragged to places he didn't want to go, but never imagined he'd be on the receiving end of such a situation.

He sat down next to her. "Sorry you had to come to Maine."

"It's not your fault."

That it wasn't. He wondered if maybe she liked a boy that was going to the party. He imagined some rich preppy kid right out of a John Hughes movie, complete with pleated khakis and a pastel sweater tied around his neck. Sam already couldn't stand the kid. He decided not to say anything more unless spoken to, so in silence, the two teenagers looked out over the bay as darkness made its way.

14

Sam woke up on the couch with the full morning sunshine blaring like synth horns. Disappointment didn't take long to make its presence felt. He had imagined talking into the night with Karla like they had years before. They would be out on the deck this time, with the radio towers smoldering in the distance. He would reach down and take her hand and fingers would entwine. Maybe there would be a kiss when parents couldn't see and younger siblings were off playing somewhere.

Sam had the wherewithal to bring a change of clothes with him into the living room, so that he would be groomed when he saw Karla. He grabbed his t-shirt and jeans and headed down to the cellar, walkman in hand. *Hysteria* was still in the deck from his bike ride the day before. Karla hated Def Leppard. Should he too? Sam pressed play anyway. 'Women' washed over him with polish and wide dynamic range. Joe Elliot's raspy testimony that he couldn't live without women made Sam feel older. The song faded out. He heard people moving above him. Sam took off his headphones and was pretty sure he heard Karla's footfall. He went over to the bookshelf and picked up an early Hardy Boys mystery book. Its painted picture cover held two boyish faces looking askance. Behind them, there was a cliff, on top of which was a beacon. Females were certainly a mystery to his coming of age mind. One was upstairs taking her place at the kitchen table. Time for him to make his way.

There sat everybody. Fathers were talking politics, mothers joined in when they saw fit. Tina and Ben were going on about who knows what. There was Karla, she had not yet dressed for the day. Sam thought she looked beautiful in her long nightdress and hair a little messed up. He turned from her and ascended the few remaining steps.

"Good morning sunshine," Gretchen said as he approached the table.

Sam's face turned red. "Good morning," he replied.

Attention was on him as he made his way to the empty seat next to Karla. He looked up to see her parents gazing at them approvingly.

"What?" she asked, embarrassed.

Sam said nothing, his face grew even redder.

The table was filled with food; fresh fruit, his mother's Spanish omelette, there were even muffins. He dug in.

It was silent until Karla turned to him somewhat excitedly. "My mom said I can go see that band with you tonight."

It was a good start to the day.

"Steve said he would let us in free," Sam told the jury of adults.

"Steve is the boyfriend of this young woman who works at the restaurant where Sam buses tables," his mother explained. "Stephanie has been good for Sam."

The last statement made him feel like a little kid. He almost said something in his defense, but couldn't think of anything. He thought about Stephanie, so beyond his reach, yet right there, listening, and helping him navigate the wiles of adolescence. When he started working at Eleanor's, Sam was still in his cocoon; now, he had been transformed. Stephanie had been a part of his life that whole time.

Brunch was done and the females headed to the mall for some last minute school shopping. The boys' father took Andrew and the boys downtown for the usual tour. They started up on the Western Promenade with its exquisite mansions overlooking Casco Bay. There were a few sailing ships out there, along with the usual gargantuan oil tankers. They rode along Commercial Street until it blossomed into beautiful brick buildings and trolley tracks still visible through cobblestones. After parking, they walked onto wharfs where fishermen plied their trade in small boats with nets and traps. The scene was familiar to the boys, but Andrew told them things about the boats that they did not know. It was interesting, but Sam's mind drifted to what was happening later on.

The low sound of the radio soundtracked the short drive to the Grange Hall. Peter Gabriel sang 'In Your Eyes' until Youssou N'dour's mysterious vocal cut through rhythm and synths. Sam couldn't understand the words, but was pretty sure they described what he was feeling in the here and now.

The car stopped just before the old wooden building constructed long ago as a place for local farmers to congregate.

"Have fun," his father said as he looked into the rearview mirror at his son.

"Okay Dad," Sam replied, not yet at the age where he knew enough to say thank you.

They stepped out of the backseat and into the dirt parking lot filled with cars. The sun was setting behind the Grange Hall in hues of yellow, orange, blue.

Up the large front steps they made their way. "Two dollars," said the young man at the door.

Sam started to reach into his pocket when he heard a

familiar voice say, "It's okay Thatcher, they're my guests." It was Stephanie. She turned her attention to the teenagers. "I was hoping you'd make it to the show." She extended her hand to Karla, "It's nice to meet you, I'm Stephanie," she said. "I hope you guys like the band. They're doing their soundcheck right now," she said, pointing toward the stage.

There was Steve behind the kit, he was hitting his snare, now his tom, bass drum; boom, boom, boom. The guitar player had a black Strat with an orange racing stripe. He was crouched over, turning the dials of pedals on the floor. Sam wondered what kind of hoodoo those rectangular metal boxes produced.

The Grange Hall looked kind of like a gymnasium without basketball hoops. Chairs lined the walls. There were a lot of people sitting, but more were standing. The crowd was older, or at least it seemed that way to Sam.

The lanky guitar player stepped up to the microphone. "Thanks for coming out," he said.

A roar went up from the assembled. "We're the Next Wave, from Portland, Maine." Irony was not lost on the crowd, some laughed, some cheered. "You might know this one."

It was Peter Gabriel again. 'Sledgehammer' this time, rocked out. Sam looked over to Karla, her eyes were closed and she was sort of dancing. Sam followed her lead. The song ended and the crowd roared loud. "Thank you," the singer said.

Karla was clapping. "These guys are better than I thought they'd be," she said.

Here he was at a concert with a beautiful girl from out of state. Never had Sam felt so cool. He caught eyes down by the stage. It was Stephanie smiling back at him. Sam's lips pushed up a grin as the Next Wave launched into one of their own. It was kind of like REM's song about the end of the world, but more disco. There was a cheer up front, they had heard this one before. Sam looked up at Steve, controlled keeper of the four on the floor. The drummer was having a blast.

They played another original before taking on a power pop version of Def Leppard's 'Photograph', complete with full harmonies.

Karla cheered and raised a fist in the air when the song was done. She turned to Sam, "Maybe not all of Def Leppard is bad."

Heat was rising inside that Grange Hall. The band slowed it down with an original ballad. Sam moved closer to Karla to see if he could get a sense of where she stood.

"This is a cool song," uttered Sam.

"Do you know it?"

"No, this is the first time I've seen them live."

"Me too," Karla joked with dimples.

"Do you have any bands like this at home?"

"My boyfriend is in a band, they were supposed to be playing at that party I'm missing."

There it was, a boyfriend. So that was it. Sam did not know how to react, so he did not.

"Well, I guess technically he's not my boyfriend, but we date. He's a senior."

There were so many messages in the sentence Karla had just uttered that Sam spent the next few songs trying to sort through them. Best he could tell, romance was out on this night. He wanted to go over and tell Stephanie. Most likely she would say that Karla had clarified that the guy was not actually her boyfriend. Stephanie would probably also tell him he could be a songwriter fronting a band on that very stage if he put his mind to it. The boy looked up at the lead singer strumming his guitar as he sang. Sam imagined himself up there. His mind drifted to his room and the closet that held his guitar.

"You want to go closer to the stage?" Karla asked Sam.

He nodded. They weaved through loosely packed people until they were near Stephanie.

"What do you think?" she asked Sam.

"Pretty cool."

"Are you having fun?" Stephanie asked Karla, who nodded her response.

Stephanie smiled before turning back to the stage. Sam looked up at Steve, who pointed a drumstick right at him.

The boy couldn't help but smile. If it weren't for the fact that Karla had said something about a boyfriend, this would have been the best night of his life, for sure.

The band played a few more, then took a break. Steve came down from the stage and hugged Stephanie in her Stevie Nicks skirt and pink Converse.

"Sam!" exclaimed the drummer. "I'm so glad you could make it."

"You guys are great."

"Thanks, we're hoping to get into the studio soon." Steve said before introducing himself to Karla. "You're hanging with a winner," he said to her.

Sam blushed, so did Karla. Neither said a word.

Steve turned his attention back to Sam. "Have you been using that tuner I gave you?"

Sam hadn't been, but he couldn't tell that to Steve. "A little," he said instead.

"Keep learning to play guitar. Todd and I are getting sick of Charlie."

"Getting sick of me, eh?" asked the lead singer.

"Yeah," Steve replied, jocularly. "We've already found your replacement."

Charlie reached out to shake the hand of his rival. "I'll watch my back," he said.

The band and their girlfriends then coalesced in a circle to discuss the first set. A couple minutes later they scattered into the crowd to thank people for coming.

Sam turned to Karla. "Do you want to go outside until they start playing again?"

"Sure."

Through the crowd they weaved their way onto the porch, where smokers stood blowing toxic fumes. They stepped down the stairs to the parking lot.

Sam thought of what to say. Should he ask her about school? Or concerts? He didn't want to ask about her so-called boyfriend, that was for sure. Sam settled on, "I wonder what Tina and Ben are doing."

Karla smiled. "Probably watching Nickelodeon."

"Probably."

The conversation turned to younger siblings and how they can be such a pain, but how they could be cool sometimes too.

The second set was about to start. Back inside they went. Sam and Karla made their way close to the stage. The Next Wave launched into Springsteen's 'Glory Days'. Sam closed his eyes and started moving to the rhythm track. Steve was a great drummer and the band followed the pace he set.

Karla was moving too, more mellow than Sam, but moving nonetheless. It remained so as the band mixed originals and covers all the way to 'And We Danced' by the Hooters.

"I love this song," Karla said, and soon they were facing each other, dancing the night away. Both kids sang every word. Sam looked at Karla, dirty blond hair once pulled into a ponytail was now loose over ears, pink lips were smiling back at him. He made a couple funny moves, she giggled and followed his lead. Sam glanced past Karla and caught eyes looking at him. It was Jessica Song. Immediately, she disappeared into the crowd. Maybe he sort of had someone too.

The song ended and the crowd sent up a roar. Karla even let out a, "Woo-hoo!"

"We'd love to do this all night, but the city has ordinances," Charlie said to spontaneous boos. "We've got one more for you."

The band launched into a rocking version of 'Raspberry Beret' and sophomore souls kept dancing away. He looked at Karla rhythmically running in place, dimples shining and eyes kind of closed. Now she was leaning from side to side. Sam followed her moves. They smiled at each other. "*Stay* cool," she said to him in exactly the right way. Sam pushed out a chuckle. Her words reminded him school was quickly approaching. That got him thinking again about Jessica. He couldn't help wonder whether she was watching, and if so, whether that was a good thing or not. The band ended the song and Karla looked at her Swatch. "It's ten," she said.

"We should probably get outside."

Sam went over to Stephanie. She hugged him. "I'm so glad you guys came."

Steve waved from the stage. "Take it easy Sam."

They made their way through the crowd. Sam kept an eye out for Jessica. He saw her friend Stacy and a couple other girls from school. Jessica though, was nowhere to be seen.

Out into the night now, Sam and Karla stepped down stairs and through the parking lot, where cars were pulling away. Up ahead was his father's brand new Taurus.

They bounced in their sneakers toward the waiting car. Each climbed in one side of the backseat. "Did you kids have a good time?" his father asked.

"Yeah," said Sam.

"Definitely," Karla added.

Off into the night they rode.

15

The families rode out to Fort Williams on Sunday. Karla was quiet as they walked amongst the ruins of the mansion long ago built and abandoned. The sky was gray with billowing clouds and the turquoise ocean was turning with white caps. Cold fog pushed in from the expanse before them. Autumn was on its way.

Sam watched as Tina and Ben climbed the rocks. It wasn't long ago that he'd be down there with them, joyfully jumping from one jutting surface to another, bending over tidal pools, pulling out little crabs and snails, thinking it was the greatest thing in the world. Now, here he was, standing next to a beautiful girl he had danced with the night before. She would soon be leaving to go back to her life, her parties, and her sort of boyfriend who was in a band. Sam had tried to start a conversation with her earlier in the day, but the Karla of Friday had returned. Here, on the water's edge, she was quiet in contemplation. Sam could only guess what was on her mind. Whatever it was, it kept either of them from saying much as they stood looking over vistas of jagged rocks and the white and turquoise of the ocean churning before them.

"This is more of what I expected Maine to look like," Karla eventually said.

"It's beautiful, isn't it?"

"Yes," she said, "yes it is."

The families then rode out to Pine Point for the obligatory seafood dinner at the Clambake. Seagulls circled, waiting for the generosity of humans.

Soon they were back home. The kids were watching MTV. 'Every Breath You Take' by the Police came on, reminding Sam of the summer of '83, when they visited Connecticut and he first saw the cable station that transformed the cultural landscape. The girl beside him was the same as that summer, but they had both sailed beyond those first waves of adolescence, like ghost ships from other ports, meeting here again in Portland.

"I still love this song," Karla said.

This time it was Sam who said nothing.

There was one long day to contemplate all this before the school year started. It was spent doing the same things he had done all summer. This time though, there was the addition of a fresh memory. Against all odds, Karla and Jessica had been in the same space and time as he; what were the chances? He thought back towards the beginning of the summer; of missing his chance to talk to Jessica at the bike rack, and then catching Karla looking at him on the lobster boat. The wide array of color behind her was similar to sunsets behind 95 as cars whizzed by while his friends played computer baseball. It was time to transition to the next phase, into the mysteries of late adolescence. He was officially no longer a sophomore, that magical age of awakening for him.

Waking up that first day of school is never easy, but then again, neither are the proceeding ones. Two months of freedom came to an end with his mother poking her head into his room and saying, "Sam, time to get up for school."

He rolled out of bed, showered, put on his new tapered acid washed jeans, and pulled an Oxford over his Bryan Adams t-shirt.

This year he would be getting a ride with Garrett. Cal was already in the shotgun seat. Sam had to settle for the back yet again. He said not a word, no one did as they pulled out on to Forest Avenue. They were all feeling pretty much the same new school year blues. All that extra time to play *Hardball*, organize baseball cards, and stay up late watching West Coast games had evaporated into the aether of time. The new school year brought excitement though; new classes, new friends, new adventures.

"Hey, I heard your girlfriend moved," Garrett said to Sam through the rearview.

"What are you talking about?"

"Jessica Song. I heard she moved to New Jersey or New York or something."

"That's impossible," Sam said, irritably. Seeing her Saturday night had pushed that possibility to the back of his mind.

"Don't get mad at me," Garrett said.

"I'm not mad at you. I saw her the other night," Sam said.

"Didn't she tell you she was moving?"

"I didn't talk to her."

"Why not?"

"I was dancing with Karla, the girl from Connecticut."

"When did all this happen?" Cal asked.

"Saturday night."

"Where?"

"At the Grange Hall?"

Garrett's house was one thousand feet away, at most. Cal's barely double that. "I didn't know they had concerts there."

"Neither did I," Sam replied.

"Why didn't you tell us?" Cal asked.

There were a lot of reasons. Foremost of which was he didn't want them to embarrass him in front of Karla. Plus, Stephanie and Steve were his friends, separate from Cal and Garrett. Sam took the high road though, and said nothing.

The silence that followed sent him meditating on the blow he had just received. It was certainly possible Jessica had moved. All the same, the fact he had recently seen her told him differently. Could it have been possible she had come into the restaurant that busy Saturday to say good-bye?

Soon they were pulling into the serpentine parking lot. Kids were milling about beside their automobiles. Trunk speakers were pumping Def Leppard and Guns N' Roses. The two together formed a cacophony that would have to do as the soundtrack to the start of junior year. The three walked up the parking lot, then in through the back doors to the controlled madness of high school. Freshmen mixed with more familiar faces. He saw Kat. She caught him unawares with a hug. "How was the rest of your summer?" she asked.

"Good."

"Mine was awesome. I told you about drama camp, right?"

"Yes."

"It was inspiring," she said like only she could. "Still

listening to Bryan Adams I see," she said, pointing at his shirt. "You really should expand your horizons."

Sam thought about how he listened to the Smiths with Karla, and saw the Next Wave just the other night. "I am," he said confidently before capitalizing on the chance he had been waiting for. "I saw you at Huey Lewis you know."

Kat's face turned red. "My mother made me go."

"I saw you dancing. It looked like you were having fun."

"Looks can be deceiving," she said, trying to sound decisive.

Sam just smiled.

Kat had other news. "Did you hear Jessica Song moved?"

There it was, for real. In the course of two days, his summer hopes faded into autumn. Kat saw someone she knew and moved on. Sam was left standing alone in the busy hallway. He looked down the long corridors and thought about the walk he had taken with Jessica. There would be no new act this year, at least it seemed that way to Sam.

The day went by in a blur. History and English were going to be fine. Algebra II looked okay; Kat was in there at least. Sam heard all about drama camp.

No one was home when Garrett dropped him off. He took out his box of 45s. Soon, Lou Gramm was singing

'Midnight Blue' over his speakers because that's how Sam thought he was feeling. Just as he was about to put the needle to the groove again, he remembered his guitar. The closet door was open, and there it sat at the center of his baseball shrine. When he took it out, the little piece of paper with Jessica's phone number fell to the floor. He picked it up. There were the familiar digits. What could he do now? He folded it up and placed it back in the box next to the tuner Steve had given him. Sam picked up the device and put it on top of the guitar. Just as Steve had told him, he turned the tuning pegs until the needle of the tuner hit the center for each string. It took him a few minutes, but when done, he was amazed at how much better the instrument sounded. E minor was where he went first. There it was, sounding sad, next he moved to a partial G, then C. He repeated the sequence, then again. The dirt road and radio towers came into his mind. It was all starting to make sense.

Jason Lambert is a schoolteacher, and aspiring musician, who grew up in the Riverton neighborhood of Portland, Maine. It took some time for him to realize just how awesome the music of the eighties was. Now, he spends a lot of time playing synthesizers to try and recreate the sounds of that decade with a project called Suns So Far... He still lives in Portland. This is his first novel.

Grace Heinig designed the blue sky background on the cover. Abbey Slinker drew the towers.